SUMMER GIRL

SUMMER GIRL

by **Deborah Moulton**

DIAL BOOKS FOR YOUNG READERS ◆ *New York*

Published by Dial Books for Young Readers
A Division of Penguin Books USA Inc.
375 Hudson Street
New York, New York 10014

Library of Congress Cataloging in Publication Data
Moulton, Deborah. Summer girl / by Deborah Moulton.
p. cm.
Summary: Because her mother is dying, Tommy is sent
to live with her estranged father, and she gradually comes to
understand him and the death of the woman they both love.
ISBN 0-8037-1153-0 (trade).
[1. Death—Fiction. 2. Fathers and daughters—Fiction.
3. Mothers and daughters—Fiction.] I. Title.
PZ7.M859Su   1992   [Fic]—dc20   91-15790   CIP   AC

To my mother, Rose Fillmore Morgan, in loving memory
D. M.

SUMMER GIRL

CHAPTER 1

Tommy gripped the battered handles of her carry-on bag and leaned her head against the window to look at the roofs of the tiny houses far below. The plane dipped and began to descend to the runway. Hard flecks of rain hit the glass and shivered backward in zig zags. Unconsciously, her hand sought the tiny heart locket that hung about her neck on its gold chain.

"Scared, honey?" asked the man seated next to her.

Tommy shook her head. "No," she answered.

"Well, gee, you're a brave little tiger, aren't you? I hate landing in the rain. And heck, I travel almost every week out to the coast. Why, last year, I made seven trips to Europe. Still can't get over that queasy feeling when a plane tries to land in the rain."

Tommy stared out the window and tried to ignore the man squashed into the seat beside her. He had bloated pink cheeks and his after-shave reeked like an open package of fruit-flavored Life Savers that had been left out in the sun too long. Was he trying to be nice? Or was he trying to pick her up? Did he realize she was only thirteen? She hated being "tall for her age." Did anyone know how humiliating it was when the seventh grade lined up and she towered over all the other kids like some kind of freak? "Doesn't your mother ever feed you?" Peter Farber once asked her. "You're the skinniest—" but that was as far as he got. Tommy punched him hard in the jaw and knocked him against the wall outside the school library. She didn't care about being skinny. Absolutely nobody, *nobody* criticized her mother, especially not when . . . but it was better not to think about that now.

The plane landed with a squealing of brakes and several bounces. The seat belt lights blinked on and off in protest, and the stewardess announced that they had landed in the Bangor airport and to please remember to take all their personal belongings and that she hoped they had had a pleasant flight.

"Fat chance," muttered Tommy as she yanked her raincoat down from the overhead compartment. The seat belt light had been on most of the trip, the plane had done a number of disturbing jolts and drops as it battled with the air currents, and she had been mashed between the window and the fat man beside her.

"Someone meeting you, honey?" he asked in an oily voice.

"My father is meeting me," snapped Tommy. "And I don't want to be the one to tell him that you keep trying to pick me up, because he's got a gun and a Doberman that eats people like you for his afternoon snack!"

"Okay, okay. Just trying to be friendly. You got a real attitude problem, missy."

Tommy glared at him and put her hands on her hips. She knew she had gone too far, as always—but she wasn't about to back down.

She waited until the man gathered his things, stepped into the aisle, and was swept along by the disembarking passengers. Then she sank back into her seat. "Oh, God, I hope he hasn't forgotten," she whispered. And what if I don't recognize him? What if he doesn't recognize me?

"Are you all right?" The voice was polite and measured.

Tommy glanced up at the stewardess. "Yes, every thing is fine, thank you." The stewardess stood over her and smiled. Then Tommy realized the plane was empty. "I'm sorry," she said and grabbed at her bag. "I guess I was daydreaming."

"I do it all the time myself," said the stewardess kindly, as she ushered Tommy out of the plane. "Is someone meeting you?"

"My father," said Tommy briskly. Why does everyone keep asking me that? she thought angrily. She nervously ran her fingers through her short blond hair that almost made her look like a boy until her fingers touched the tiny gold earrings that her mother had given her. Then she straightened the belt of her jeans and took a deep breath. Her heart had started pounding, and she could feel her face turning red. Clenching the handles of her bag in her fist she strode down the accordion corridor into the terminal.

There was a man waiting by the gate. He was older than she remembered, or at least older than the photograph she kept in her secret drawer. His blue plaid flannel shirt was dirty and tucked into a faded pair of green work pants that were torn at the knee. His face was wrinkled and there were dark circles under his eyes. His hair was white.

Tommy stood before him. Then she shrugged her shoulders and said, "Hi. I'm here." The name thing was something they would have to sort out. What do you call your father whom you haven't seen since you were three years old and don't remember anything about?

"So you're Tommy."

"Yeah."

"Do you have any other bags?"

"Yeah. I checked it through. Well, I didn't know how long I was going to be here. And so I took most of my stuff." She did not want her father thinking she always traveled with a huge suitcase large enough for a family of ten. "How'd you recognize me?" she asked.

"Your Aunt Bareeba sent me a picture. Besides, it wasn't that hard. You were the only kid on the plane."

"Oh. Yeah." Tommy felt a wave of disappointment sweep over her. Why couldn't he say something like, "Of course I'd know my own daughter anywhere!" Fat chance. What do you expect from a father who didn't even remember your birthday or Christmas or anything, never even called, and hadn't seen you in ten years?

They claimed her bag in silence. It was a huge green-and-black checkered monstrosity, and Tommy felt acutely embarrassed as she pointed it out. It had been Aunt Bareeba's, actually. "It's just the thing, Tommy," Tommy heard herself mimicking Aunt Bareeba in her head. "You can fit all your clothes and 'valubles' in it. Don't say I don't do nothing for you. I can't tell you how many places this old suitcase has been. But it looks like I won't be traveling for a while. So I'm happy to give it to you. Just the thing for clothes and 'valubles.' " Aunt Bareeba's idea of valuables, or 'valubles,' was anything that you owned. It also was a vague term that encompassed certain areas of the human body. "You'll have to leave the room now, Tommy. I'm going to wash your mother's valubles."

"It's all right, Bareeba. I can wash myself later. I'm not that weak yet." Mom had laughed gently. But she held on to Tommy's hand and gave it the secret squeeze that meant *I love you.*

Tommy found herself blinking hard. There was a tightness behind her eyes that made her whole face hurt.

"This is my truck. You'll have to put your bag in the back. Looks like a Bareeba special to me."

"Yeah." Tommy felt a rush of relief that her father had recognized the bag immediately as Aunt Bareeba's. Maybe everything would work out, maybe. She glanced at the man beside her. His hair was thin and just a little too long in the back so that the ends bent as they touched his dirty blue shirt collar. I doubt it, she thought bitterly.

They drove along in silence for a while. Tommy watched the passing pine trees and the granite boulders that sometimes flanked the road like broken teeth. The truck smelled of fish and cigarette smoke. The rain spattered heavy drops on the windshield. The wipers squeaked and sighed as they swung back and forth.

Aunt Bareeba had no right to send her away, not now. "It's for your own good, sweetie," said Aunt Bareeba in a firm no-nonsense "nurse" voice. "You don't want to see your mother going through this. It's not right for a girl your age. Besides, I just can't take care of two people. I'm not as young as I used to be. I'm worn to the bone with your mother's illness, just worn to the bone, and I don't need a teenager underfoot. This will give you the chance to get to know your father. Believe me, you'll thank me for all I've done some day."

Dream on, Aunt Bareeba. "How much farther?" Tommy asked.

" 'Bout another hour. Maybe more." The man sighed. "Mind if I smoke?"

Tommy shrugged her shoulders. "Sure. Go right ahead." Actually, she despised the smell of cigarette smoke, especially in cars. It made her want to puke. She opened her window and let the cold, wet air play against her face.

The man glanced at her. "Guess I won't," he said.

"No. It's okay. I don't mind."

There was an embarrassing silence, and Tommy felt obligated to crank the window shut.

The man took a deep breath. "I guess this is kind of tough on both of us."

Tommy shrugged her shoulders and didn't answer.

"And you have to call me something."

"What do you mean?" Tommy asked cautiously.

"Well, I was thinking in the airport. Well, actually, when I got your Aunt Bareeba's letter. I mean you got to call me something."

"What?"

"When you were a little thing, you called me Daddy."

"I don't remember that."

The man cleared his throat. "I figured you wouldn't," he said. "So I figured you might as well call me Jud. That's what everyone else does. Except the men at the yard sometimes call me Judge, but that's kind of a joke."

"Okay."

That was the end of the conversation for the rest of the trip. Somewhere between Bangor and Ellsworth, Tommy found her eyes closing and her head resting on the window. She was so tired. And it seemed she had been so tired for so long. Lying awake in her dark room, waiting in case her mother called her or needed her. Trying so hard during the day to be helpful and quiet and good, and still Aunt Bareeba sent her away. First the dog to the kennel, and now her to her father's. Poor Dozer, he hated cages. And how could he be expected to understand? He was just a dumb dog.

The truck stopped short with a jerk. Tommy opened her eyes to see what might eventually be her home. The house was small with peeling pale green paint and shutters that perhaps once had been white but were now worn down to the bare wood. There was a shed farther back on the property that seemed to be in a state of partial collapse with some farm equipment rusting in front of it. A small rocky field separated the house from its neighbor, which seemed to be in much the same condition. Across the street was a gas station with two ancient-looking pumps and, beside it, a small general store with a dark wooden porch. In the distance, a McDonald's in pristine condition sported its famed golden arches in defiance of the poverty and seediness that surrounded it.

"You going to get out?" asked Jud.

"I don't remember this at all," said Tommy in a low voice. Slowly she opened the door and stepped into the rain.

"No reason you would. I had to sell the house on the shore. The taxes were pretty bad, and those summer people just keep driving up the land prices like crazy. I've been renting here. It suits my needs fine. I guess you're used to more."

"No, this is fine," said Tommy.

Jud hefted the Bareeba special from the back of the pickup. "The place is kind of a mess. I figured I'd have time to clean it up a bit, but they got short-handed at the yard."

The front door opened into a dark, messy living room, beyond which Tommy could see the kitchen with a rusty sink full of unwashed dishes.

"Your room's upstairs. Mine's off the living room. We'll have to share the bathroom. There's only one in the house. I guess I ought to start looking for a bigger place."

"No. This is fine, really." Tommy's voice was numb. She followed Jud up the narrow stairs. This was turning out worse than her worst nightmares. What would her room be like? Probably full of rats and spiders with a smelly army cot against the wall and things crawling on the walls and in the corners. Get ahold of yourself, you'll manage somehow, she whispered inside her head.

Jud opened the door and motioned for Tommy to enter. Tommy gasped. The room was small, as she had known it would be, with a slanted ceiling. The wallpaper was faded, with a pattern that might once have been roses. But to her amazement there were pretty lace curtains hanging in the windows and a new lace bedspread on the bed. And the room was spotlessly clean and bright! It looked as if it belonged to another house. It even smelled faintly of pine detergent.

Jud sighed and put the Bareeba special down slowly. "Well, I guess I'll let you unpack. I'll be downstairs. I tried to fix it up so you'd like it . . . some, at least. I know you're upset about your mother. You probably don't want to talk about it. I'm really not one for talking either, but I'll do the best I can about . . . being here . . . if you . . ." His words became slower and slower until they finally stopped altogether like a broken toy. Then he just stared helplessly at Tommy for a second before turning and rubbing the door frame with his callused fingers, as if he was cleaning it or feeling for hidden splinters.

She didn't answer him. What could she say? Yes, my mother is dying. DYING! But it's not something I want to talk about. *And* I've been sent here to this awful place just because you're my father—as if that gives you special rights—not that you've ever been a real father. So GO AWAY! JUST GO AWAY! Tommy didn't say these things. She screamed them—inside her head, so loud they made her head hurt, but on the outside her face was frozen.

Jud stared at her for a moment, then backed out of the tiny room and closed the door behind him. Tommy stood with the hideous black-and-green checkered suitcase beside her. She looked at the almost new white bureau, the lace curtains, and the tiny closet complete with a few hangers. Then she noticed the tiny bedside table on which stood a small vase full of freshly cut meadow flowers. She covered her face with her hands, threw herself on the bed, and cried long and hard.

When she lifted her head, the room was dark.

She rubbed her eyes and yawned. Somewhere between sobs and tears, she must have fallen asleep.
She had a headache and her mouth tasted stale. She
reached for the lamp and turned it on.

The house was quiet. When she peered out of her
door, the stairs were dark. Jud must have gone out.
I need some Excedrin, she thought. Except for her
pounding headache, the rest of her body felt numb,
almost cold from all the crying. The Excedrin was
packed somewhere in the Bareeba special. It was a
relief that Jud immediately recognized the suitcase
as a gift from Aunt Bareeba. And he had really tried
to fix up the bedroom for her.

Tommy nibbled the fingernail of her fourth finger
thoughtfully—careful not to bite it off—even though
the edge was temptingly ragged. It would be so easy
to bite just a little harder. . . . She took a sharp
breath. No. Mom had been so proud when she
stopped biting her nails. She took the finger firmly
out of her mouth and shoved her hand hard into
her pocket.

And she didn't want to be friends with Jud either.
Sure the room looked nice. But that didn't make up
for ten years of no letters, no birthday cards, not
even a phone call. It didn't make up for kids at school
talking about their fathers and she'd had nothing to
say—just standing on the outskirts of the circle, or
all of a sudden remembering she had something else
to do—just so somebody wouldn't ask her a ques-

tion. It would have been easier if he'd been dead. Then people wouldn't ask stupid things like, What does he look like? What does he do? Don't you miss him? In first and second grades she would talk a lot about visiting him on vacations—hoping that it would come true, hoping that she would visit him and get to know him—that he would call or write and then she wouldn't have to lie anymore. She even rehearsed a scene over and over in her head as she was going to sleep about him coming to see her at school and holding out his arms to her like other kids' fathers. And everybody staring and realizing she really did have a father. It was a stupid dream. Jud never came to see her. He never even sent her a letter—not even a postcard. So you can just forget the father-daughter bit, Jud, she thought angrily. Because I'm not buying it. Not for a minute.

Tommy unpacked slowly and carefully. It wasn't clothes that took up all the room, it was all the other stuff—her hair dryer, her photo album, Bartel Bear, her favorite pillow, her makeup that Aunt Bareeba said made her look like a tart, and the picture of her mother in its carved wood frame. She put that on the night table beside her bed and then shifted it several times to make sure the angle was right.

She looked at her watch and realized she was hungry. There must be something to eat in that filthy kitchen. But when she gathered up enough courage to leave the safety of her room, descend the narrow stairs, and pick her way through the gloomy living room, the sight of the dishes still piled in the rusty old sink was enough to take away anyone's appetite. Uncertain as to what to do next, she stood in the kitchen and surveyed the mess. A small area of the dining table had been cleared, and a note lay there. It was for her.

Tommy—I'm going to get some dinner.
I'll be back soon.

JUD

P. S. Bareeba called. Said not to call back.
Your mother was sleeping.

Tommy slammed the note back down. The familiar rage was building inside her. It was almost as if Aunt Bareeba was being greedy about her mom's sickness. It was as if she was trying to separate her mother from her own daughter. Well, she's not going to, thought Tommy defiantly. I'll write Mom every day, maybe even twice a day. And good letters, not sad letters. I'll make her really proud of me. And if I have to, I'll run away from here, and I'll get back there somehow, just to see her again.

The pink stationery kit was in the top drawer in her room. There was even a pen with it and envelopes. It was a birthday present she had never used.

Carefully, she lifted the lid, snapped the paper

ribbon that was tied around the writing paper, and smoothed out a sheet of paper.

Dear Mom,

Tommy paused and chewed on the end of the pen. Then she settled herself on her stomach, with her legs dangling off the bed so that she could write more comfortably. She wanted this to be a good letter and not sad. Something that would make her mother smile. The dying part—that must never be mentioned. Sometimes it seemed as if it wouldn't happen or that the doctors had made a mistake and if you didn't say anything about it, it faded.

A world without Mom in it just didn't seem possible. Tommy clutched the pen firmly.

I got here safe and sound. Jud seems OK. He's older than the picture you gave me. He recognized me right away.

Guess what? He has a new house. Actually it isn't his. It's rented. He sold the house on the shore that we used to live in—something about taxes, I think. He seems really nice. He fixed up my bedroom and even put fresh flowers by my bed. He took one look at my suitcase and knew right away that Aunt Bareeba had given it to me. He called it a Bareeba special!!!!

I think we're going to get on fine. The house is

great. It even has a little shed, and there's a Mc-
Donald's on the corner. Don't worry, Mom, I promise I'll eat healthy stuff too.

Bartel Bear is sitting on my bed. He's still leaking
sawdust all over the place. He says he misses you,
and he's furious with Aunt Bareeba for calling him a
smelly bear and full of dirty germs. He would much
rather be in his old place on the foot of your bed
and guarding you. He says if he wasn't a stuffed an-
imal bear, he would bite Aunt Bareeba. I can't say I
blame him.

Well, I'd better go. Jud has fixed this incredible
dinner—like you wouldn't believe—for my first night
here. I really miss you, Mom. And I think about you
all the time. But I'm going to be okay, so please don't
worry about me.

I love you,
Tommy

P.S. I'm *not* sending love to Aunt Bareeba. She said I
wasn't to call you because you were sleeping. It's my
first night away, and I think that's really mean of her.
So there. But I'm going to try and write you a lot.
You don't have to write me back if you don't feel like
it. I'll understand. Anyway, I love you. 'Bye for now.

Tommy

The front door slammed. Tommy jumped off the
bed and opened the door to her room. It was Jud.

She could hear him moving about the place. Slowly, she came down the stairs.

"You woke up," observed Jud. He was sweeping a place clear on the dining room table with his arm. When he had finished, he put the bag of groceries down and went into the kitchen.

"Where were you?" asked Tommy.

"I went to the deli. Didn't you see my note?"

"Yeah. It's just you were gone a long time."

"Well, Cleo's was shut, so I had to drive up to Bordman's. I got a barbecued chicken and some coleslaw. You like coleslaw, don't you?"

"Yeah, sure."

"What do you drink? Milk? Soda? I talked to Lida Barnaby down the street when I knew you was coming, and she said to get lots of soda because that was what her boys used to drink when they was your age. So I got a six-pack of Coke. That okay?"

"Sure. Anything." Jud's ungrammatical way of speaking set Tommy's teeth on edge. God, I hate Maine accents, she thought.

They ate the chicken in silence. Jud mostly stared at his plate. Tommy watched him thoughtfully. He really looked old. More like somebody's grandfather. His hair was thin and white, and the creases around his mouth and eyes made him look as if he was always frowning. His fingernails were dirty. He smelled faintly of cigarette smoke and sweat. Tommy

remembered he had said he worked in "the yard."
Maybe it was a lumberyard. He was slouching over
his plate. Tommy found herself unconsciously
straightening her own shoulders and cutting her
portion of chicken in a way that would make even
Aunt Bareeba proud.

Jud pushed back his plate with a sigh. "That's that,"
he said. "Usually I just fix myself something out of a
can or grab a burger up at the McDonald's. But I
figured it was your first night here and you ought to
eat good. Sorry I took so long but, like I said, Cleo's
was closed so I had to drive up to Bordman's Deli,
and that's a good twenty miles from here."

"The chicken was delicious, Jud. You want me to
help clear?"

"Nope . . . I usually leave it till the morning." He
looked at her thoughtfully. "Guess I'll go outside for
my smoke."

"That's okay," said Tommy quickly. "You don't
have to."

But Jud had already pushed through the screen
door. Tommy watched him take a few steps away
from the house and reach in his pocket for his cigarettes. There was a flash of flame from his lighter.
Then he stood facing the street, the tip of the cigarette glowing red in the night. When it finally
burned to the very end, he flicked the butt away and
put his hands in his pockets and just stood there.

Tommy thought she saw him turn once back to the house, but it may have been because he was reaching for another cigarette. She saw the flash of the lighter and again the red glow in the dark.

This is great, she thought bitterly as she moved away from the window. My father can't stand being around me. He doesn't even want to talk to me.

I could always run away, I really could. The beginnings of a plan began to form. I'd need a map, and I'd have to hitchhike part of the way. Twenty-four dollars and seventy-two cents sure wouldn't buy a bus ticket from Bradenpond, Maine, to Stapleton, Illinois.

And Jud would never even notice I was gone. How could he? He doesn't notice anything. He doesn't even care about the filth around him.

But then why would he fix up the bedroom? None of it made any sense at all. She looked at the dinner plates with their bones and congealing chicken grease and shivered. "Night, Jud," she called through the screen door.

Jud turned slowly to the house. "Night, Tommy," he replied. "I'll be in later." Then he turned back again to watch the road.

Tommy tramped slowly up the stairs and into the oasis of her room where she sat on the edge of her bed and stared at the wallpaper. She found her fingers drumming a bored tune on the stationery set.

No TV. No books. Not even a radio. It was going to be a long summer . . . if she stayed.

And I miss my friends, she thought wistfully. She tried to picture what Sheila Morton and Marcia Wilcox were doing. Marcia would probably be sitting on Sheila's bed, and they would have rented a movie and Sheila's mom would have made popcorn. Across the hall, Sheila's younger brother would be glued to his computer games. There would be a dance at the Youth Center in about a week. Maybe Peter Farber would come. But if she wasn't there, maybe he would dance with Sheila instead, and Sheila was supposed to be her best friend! Cold knots of jealousy began twisting up through her stomach. The guilt from being jealous—of her best friend no less— made the sick feeling worse. It was just that Sheila was so pretty with her long golden hair, and she always knew what to say to boys. She fit in. Whereas I . . . thought Tommy glumly.

Then she winced as another wave of guilt washed over her. Her mother was dying and she was worrying about fitting in?

Is there something wrong with me? she wondered. How can I be so shallow? It's not the friends, it's not the stuff I'm missing. I just wish I were home, that's all. Tommy pushed her face hard into her pillow. She wasn't crying, exactly. But her throat kept making strange harsh noises that were silenced in the softness of the pillow.

The trip with all of its uncertainties had taken its toll. Although she had convinced herself that she could never sleep in this horrible house, so far from her mother, sleep came quickly.

She woke to the sound of a bird twittering louder than any alarm clock right outside her window. The sunlight streaming in made rectangular designs on the polished wooden floor. The lace curtains heaved and billowed in the breeze. The rain and mist of the day before had vanished, and the sky was a lovely brilliant blue.

After a long steamy shower and a hair wash, Tommy ran down the stairs. Her wet hair was slicked back and still dripping on her collar. Her face felt tingly and clean, and the ends of her fingers were pink and wrinkly from the hot water.

"Morning, Jud," she called. But the house was empty. Another note lay on the dining table.

Gone to the yard. Back around 4:00.
Do whatever you like. Lida Barnaby said she'd
be dropping by later to check on you.

Jud

CHAPTER
2

Tommy looked with disgust at the plates of chicken still sitting on the table. Her wonderful sense of good feeling was quickly evaporating. How can anyone live like this? she asked herself. Well, *I'm* not going to.

Grimly, she took the plates to the kitchen and for a moment stood perplexed as to where to start. The sink was already filled with dirty dishes. The small counter beside the sink had several screwdrivers and some fishing line on it, and there was no evidence of a garbage pail anywhere. She swept the tools to one side, and stacked the plates. Where were the cleaning supplies kept? Sponges? Detergent? Soap? Anything?

It wasn't until she explored the shed that she found more or less what she wanted: a scrub brush, some Pine Sol, a sponge, dish detergent, window cleaner, and a spray bottle of Fantastik. The garbage cans were located by the shed also.

Three hours later, the kitchen was passable. The dining table had been cleared and cleaned. The papers were stacked neatly at one end. Tommy began to feel faint with hunger. She looked at her watch. Eleven-thirty. She hadn't even had breakfast.

She opened the refrigerator hoping to find something edible but realized to her dismay that another huge job lay ahead of her. The inside of the refrigerator was filthy. The only thing it contained was a selection of opened cans—some more recently opened than others, a half pint of heavy cream, a jar of relish, a jar of mayonnaise, an open package of bologna, and, at the bottom, several cans of Coke.

By the time she had walked up to McDonald's, the menu had been switched from Egg McMuffins to Big Macs. "I can let you have the juice," said the waitress in her thick Maine accent. "But we stopped servin' breakfast. Most people come in 'round six or so. The lunch crowd's startin' to show up now."

"I'm a late sleeper," answered Tommy. Then she smiled. "But thanks." She took the juice container, coffee, and hamburger back to her table.

The McDonald's seemed luxurious and antiseptically clean when compared with Jud's house. No matted-down dust balls that had to be pried out from corners, no mold growing in strange places, and no multilegged bugs darting out from under the sink.

Tommy sipped her coffee slowly. She had started drinking coffee two years ago when Aunt Bareeba said caffeine would stunt her growth. Embarrassed at always being the tallest kid in her class, she had hoped the coffee would help. To her extreme disappointment, however, she kept right on growing.

She stared through the crystal clear windows beyond the dingy houses and the winding patched road as if straining for a glimpse of her mother, hundreds of miles away.

All the thoughts that had been numbed by the Herculean task of cleaning the kitchen began filtering back. Was her mother weaker this morning? Had she passed a good night? Immediately, Tommy felt guilty because she had slept soundly—the first sound sleep in weeks.

Reluctantly, she pulled her thoughts back to the present. Just how was she going to survive a summer with Jud? Let alone *live* with him on a permanent basis!

What kind of a father was he anyway? What kind of person? All he left was a short note saying he was at work—no number to call if there was an emergency. What was she supposed to do while he was away? And who was Lida Barnaby? Well, at least I can clean up the house, she decided. Besides, anything was better than sitting around and thinking and worrying.

"Is there a post office or a mail box somewhere around here?" she asked the waitress who had given her the orange juice.

The waitress toyed thoughtfully with the collar of her uniform. "Well, there's a regular post office in Bradenpond proper," (she pronounced it "proppa"). "This here is North Bradenpond really, if you was to give it a name, that is. But there's a box down the street at the general store, and Mrs. White, she usually has stamps for sale if you ask her."

"Thanks," said Tommy. She pushed back her chair and headed for the door.

The waitress walked with her companionably and held the door open for her. "You're not from around here, are you?" The question was actually a cross between a question and a statement, and the "here" came out as "hee-ah."

"Not really," said Tommy as she let the door close behind her. "Not if I can help it," she muttered.

She mailed the letter in the post box outside the general store. There were several older people standing around on the wooden porch talking, who stared at her curiously. Tommy felt her cheeks begin to burn and flush. She kept her eyes on the ground and stuffed her hands in her pockets as she walked away quickly. "Bunch of nosy buzzards!" she muttered as she kicked a stone hard and sent it bouncing into the road.

The sign over the door of the gas station read HENRY JALLOP—AUTO MECHANIC—JALLOP & JALLOP—SINCE 1923.

Sure looks it, thought Tommy sourly. The pumps belonged in a museum, and the inside of the shop was more like an extension of the general store. There was even a row of Johnson & Johnson Band-Aids on a high shelf. Everything was dusty, and the sun filtering in through the window made the room seem as if it was filled with yellow haze.

Henry Jallop himself sold her the map. He was a skinny old man who stood very straight. His dark-blue uniform was immaculate, and it had bright yellow lettering. HENRY JALLOP—OWNER. He took the map proudly out of a box that looked as if it was a hundred years old. "Not too many people buy maps. But I stock them just in case. I try and stock everything. You never know. That's a dollar. Oh, don't bother about the tax. Doesn't seem worth it for a dollar, does it now? Where's your car?"

Tommy shrugged her shoulders. "I don't have a car."

"Puttin' the cart before the horse, isn't it? I can remember when people used horses more. In fact, I can remember my dad taking me to school in the farm cart every mornin'. Of course, in the winter we used the sleigh. Seems we got more snow back then. Don't know why that would be. You don't remember what it was like. You're too young. Are you old enough to drive?"

Do people ever stop talking around here? Tommy wondered. She took the map. "Thanks." She waved as she left.

"Take care of yourself, now," Henry called after her.

Back at Jud's, she tackled the refrigerator until she heard the front door slam and a female voice call out, "Yoo-hoo, is anybody home?" It was Lida Barnaby.

Lida Barnaby turned out to be motherly, stout, and in her mid-sixties. She had white hair, neatly coifed in a hair net, and wore a flowered dress. She brought a small black-and-white TV. "It was in the boys' room, but it doesn't get used anymore. I thought you might like it."

"Thank you," said Tommy. "I'll ask my father if I can set it up in the living room."

"Your father's been livin' alone for a long time. He doesn't really know about being a father. In fact, between you and me, he's not very good at being with people either. Lots of people around here think he's kind of peculiar,"—again the Maine accent made the words sound different. "Peculiar" had become "peculiah"—"but he works hard and he's honest, and that's more than you can say for a lot of men these days." Mrs. Barnaby sighed.

Tommy traced her finger on the dining table. She had fixed Mrs. Barnaby a cup of tea, which sat hardly touched. Peculiar? she wondered. Her stomach felt hollow and clammy inside. What did that mean? Jud was some kind of weirdo ax murderer, like on a TV movie, and the daughter would be the last to know? And there would be all sorts of horrible clues lying around that she wouldn't see until it was too late? "Why do people think he's so . . . strange?" she asked as calmly as possible.

"Oh, just that your father doesn't talk much. He talks to me because my sister Ellen knew him back before he married your mother. What a handsome boy he was too. All the girls chased him. He talked then and laughed. Smart too. Always did real well in school. He could have gone to college, you know, but he didn't have much money, and his father was sick. What a shame. He's one of those people that could have been somebody. But what are you gonna do? I guess you're worried about your mother, ain't ya?"

Tommy nodded. Well, at least Jud wasn't an ax murderer. Mrs. Barnaby didn't make him sound really weird—just sort of sad.

And anyway, Mom's being sick wasn't anybody's business—especially not Mrs. Barnaby's! Why were people always so greedy for details about her mother? Even the guidance counselor at school was always prying.

"Oh, gosh, Mrs. Barnaby. Look at the time. I promised my mother I'd call her every day." She swept up Mrs. Barnaby's full (and now quite cold) cup of tea and carried it to the sink.

Lida Barnaby took the hint. "Of course, dear. I have to be on my way. I have so many errands to do today it would make your head spin. But I'll keep checking up on you. Jud's a good man, but he's not very used to being a father, if you know what I mean."

It was five-thirty when Jud returned. He surveyed the kitchen quietly. "Gee, Tommy," he mumbled, "you needn't have gone to all this trouble."

"It wasn't any trouble, Jud. I didn't have anything else to do."

"Lida said it might get kind of lonesome for a girl your age. Did she drop by?"

"Yeah. She brought a TV. Can I put it in the living room?"

Jud shrugged his shoulders. "Sure."

"Great. It's only a black and white."

"I don't watch TV myself. She must have brought it over for you."

"She seemed nice," said Tommy slowly.

"She means well. She usually cleans up my kitchen 'bout once a month or so. Says I'm a health hazard to the neighborhood."

Tommy shifted uneasily. She found herself agreeing with Mrs. Barnaby entirely, and she wondered again, as she had wondered repeatedly through the day, how could anyone live like this? Peculiar. It was a good word. But it was *not* how you would want to describe a relative, let alone your father.

"Well, I guess I got used to getting by," Jud said apologetically, as if in answer to her thoughts. "It seemed a bit stupid to keep washing things that just got dirty again, 'specially if it was only for me." He paused thoughtfully. "But I can't have you spending your summer cleaning the house. We'll work something out somehow, I guess."

"I don't mind," said Tommy. Except she did. She minded a lot, and not just about the dirt either. Why did Aunt Bareeba send her away? The doctor said that by September, November at the latest, her mother would be dead, and the dying would be painful. Of course, it took him longer to say that. His speech was chock-full of medical jargon: where and how cancer spread through the body, diagrams, X rays. It seemed it was okay for doctors to say horrible things as long as they used a lot of technical terms—as if that would make the horribleness more manageable, more understandable. And maybe it did for the doctors.

But what about the patients? What about me? What about *my* mother?

She thought about the map carefully hidden in her top drawer. "I'll get home somehow, Mom," she whispered.

Hello, Mom,

It's 4:00 now, and Jud will be back any minute. I'm sitting on my bed looking out the window. Beyond the field, there's a pine forest, and it looks as if it goes on forever and ever.

I met a woman today, Lida Barnaby, who said she knew Jud because her sister had gone out with him before he married you. She lives down the street and has grown sons.

I really miss you, Mom, and I'm worried about you. I tried to call you earlier today, but Aunt Bareeba said you were sleeping. Please call me. I think I will go crazy if I don't hear your voice.

Anyway, I'm really trying hard. I cleaned up the kitchen and did the dishes today while Jud was at the yard. I even made Mrs. Barnaby a cup of tea when she dropped by. It must have been good tea. It was rather difficult to get her to leave.

Love and kisses.
I miss you, Mom.
Tommy.

Tommy drew a few smile faces and hearts at the bottom of the letter, slipped it into the pink envelope, and sealed it carefully. Then, sighing, she held the envelope and stared at it a few minutes before laying it down carefully on her bedside table.

The first week fell into a pattern that made Tommy feel more lonely and isolated than ever. Jud left for work at 5:30. The "yard" had turned out to be a boat yard, and Jud was a ship's carpenter—which meant that he painted and scraped and repaired, and there were always oil stains on his clothes and stains under his fingernails.

Every morning Tommy woke to an empty house, ate a bowl of cold cereal, and cleaned the kitchen. She kept her own room so neat that even Aunt Bareeba would have had no criticisms. However, the house was small, and even though the work had seemed monumental at first, once the initial filth was cleared out, cleaning the small rooms took only a couple of hours. Besides, the door to Jud's room remained shut. Tommy never opened it.

That left the rest of the day for thinking. Somehow watching television, simply because there was nothing else to do, was unsatisfying at best. Besides, only two channels came in clearly, and they played an unending succession of game shows. She wrote letters frequently. She tried reading, but there were few books around the house, and the only library was in Bradenpond proper. She bought magazines at the general store and threw her energy into filling out questionnaires and quizzes that had nothing to do with her, ones that supposedly told you if you had a successful marriage, or whether an office affair could actually help you and your spouse deal with the marital responsibilities of children.

She counted and recounted her money every day. Twenty dollars and change left. She unfolded the map carefully and studied it by the hour. Home seemed very far away. She argued continually with herself. If I run away, Jud will call Mom, and then Mom will worry and get sicker. If I don't run away, I'll go crazy. I've got to get home, but how?

At least there was food in the house. The second night Jud had driven her to a twenty-four hour supermarket in Bradenpond proper. He frowned a little when the bill came to more than one hundred dollars, but Tommy insisted that they have at least "the basics" on hand.

In the last two years her mother had been too tired to clean their little house or even shop for groceries, and Tommy had ended up being the one to run the house and buy the groceries. Weaving the metal shopping cart through the aisles reminded Tommy of her mother and the time before Aunt Bareeba came to "help out," only it was more like "take over!"

Before, Aunt Bareeba had been a figure seen only at Christmas or passing through for a brief visit in the summer. Tommy had always dreaded the arrival (or was it invasion?) of Aunt Bareeba, dressed in

enormous pantsuits and wielding the inevitable huge
suitcase and two shopping bags. It seemed impossible that she could be her mother's sister. Her own
mother was so thin and delicate, with large thoughtful
eyes. Aunt Bareeba's eyes were tiny and hidden behind thick glasses. She was always saying things like,
"Bogey, you can't possibly cook chicken like that!
I've never heard of such a thing in all my life!" Then,
turning to Tommy, "Your mother, my dear, was never
a cook, oh my goodness, no! I was the cook of the
family, wasn't I, Bogey dear?"

Mom, who was called Elaine by all her friends,
had explained that her nickname in the family was
"Bogey" because she looked so much like Humphrey
Bogart when she was a baby. There was a faded
picture on the mantel at home of Uncle Pete, age
four, holding the hand of Aunt Bareeba, a fat three-
year-old with frizzy dark hair and a scowlly expression. In a stroller, and so swaddled up with
blankets that you could see only her nose, was Mom.
Uncle Pete, only a year older than Bareeba, couldn't
say "Barbara" when he first started talking. Try as he
might, all that came out was "Bareeba."

Tommy shuddered whenever Aunt Bareeba called
her mother Bogey. To make matters worse, Bareeba
seemed to get a special thrill out of screeching, "Bogey! Bogey!" across a crowded supermarket or, worse,
on the steps at school.

Then Aunt Bareeba would describe in vivid detail the care she had given to one of her patients. Aunt Bareeba was a registered nurse in private practice. Her specialty was the old and dying. Sometimes Tommy wondered if Aunt Bareeba was so used to ordering around her patients that she just ordered around the rest of the world as well.

If they drove somewhere, Bareeba would say, "Good heavens, Bogey, you almost went through that light. I can't believe you would drive like that with a child in the car. I'd better do the driving while I'm here. You know, Tamara, your mother was never very good at driving. I drive all the time. It's part of my job. The agency gets lots of requests for nurses who drive. Bogey, why on earth do you persist in calling Tamara Tommy? It's a boy's name. I think you should call her Tammie." This was one of Bareeba's causes.

"I hate the name Tammie," growled Tommy.

"Well, if you ask me—not that it's any of my business, Lord no—I just think . . ."

You're right, it's not your business, you fat old cow, quipped Tommy inside her head. Whenever she was really angry she said a lot of things inside her head that no one heard.

"Oh, Bareeba, Jud and I just slipped into calling Tommy 'Tommy.' "

"It's my name." Tommy smiled sweetly at Bareeba. The smile might have worked if Tommy hadn't decided to jazz it up by batting her eyes at the same time. Bareeba muttered about the rudeness of the younger generation for more than an hour.

Tommy always felt ecstatic when Bareeba's visit was over and it was time for her to go take care of another poor aging invalid. They probably die just to get away from her, thought Tommy inside her head.

Then came the awful time when Tommy's mother finally went to the doctor to find out why she was so tired and why she couldn't eat anything. The tests that followed were humiliating and exhausting. Tommy went with her mother because there were only the two of them. There was no one else.

"I'd like to discuss the results with you, Mrs. Kingston," the doctor said in a very bedside manner, and immediately they both knew that something was very wrong. Mom put her arm around Tommy. "Alone, Mrs. Kingston," said the doctor with a meaningful raise of his eyebrows.

But Elaine Kingston smiled gently. "No, I'd like my daughter with me. We're in this together." Tommy felt the tears running down her cheeks. She had never loved her mother more than that moment. In the doctor's office, Elaine held Tommy's hand while the doctor told them the facts.

A few days later, Bareeba arrived to "take charge."

She was a trained nurse. She would care for her dear sister in her final illness. And she wouldn't charge a penny, not a penny. It was a matter of family duty.

Tommy was ordered to stay out of the way and limit her visits with her mother. Then after a month had gone by and school was getting out for the summer, Bareeba decided that this was the time for Tommy to get to know her father. "It's unhealthy for any thirteen-year-old to spend the summer waiting for God's hand to strike."

Tommy knew she was too old for nightmares. But after Aunt Bareeba said that, she dreamed constantly about her mother dying and screaming as she was "struck" with pain.

Finally, the first letter came. Tommy recognized her mother's handwriting immediately. It was squashy looking, with fat loops on the *l*s and *b*s. The envelope was heavy, as if there was a lot in it. Eagerly, she tore it open.

Darling,

I'm so glad you're settling in so well with your father. I don't want you to worry. Aunt Bareeba is taking very good care of me.

I'm very, very proud of you. I'm sending you a great big hug. I loved your letter. It made me laugh—especially about the "Bareeba special," but that bet-

ter be our secret. We mustn't hurt Aunt Bareeba's
feelings. She means well. I love you with all my heart.

Tommy, there is so much I want to tell you. I
thought at first we would be talking a lot on the
telephone, but Bareeba is so strict about long distance.

I don't know quite where to begin.

I keep thinking of Pete. He was the oldest. Then
came Bareeba, then me. He would be thirty-four now,
if he hadn't been killed in Vietnam.

Bartel Bear was a present from Pete when I was
four and he was seven. He saved up for it and used
all the money in his piggy bank to buy me a teddy
bear—just because his best friend's baby sister had a
teddy bear and he didn't want me to feel left out.

I can still see him now with his funny short crew
cut. In fact, whenever he came back from the barber, you could see his pink scalp shine in the sun
through the white prickles of his hair. The other
kids teased him and called him egghead.

By the time he was ten, his silvery hair had dark-
ened to a grayish brown. At fourteen, he stopped
going to the barber. His hair became thick and wavy.
He brushed it often and continuously "borrowed" my
shampoo and conditioner. But I didn't mind. I loved
Pete and would have given him anything.

At that time, it seemed that Poppa was always
yelling at him. Sometimes he would slam his can of
beer down so hard that foamy drops would shower
the den in a sticky mess.

Meanwhile, Bareeba wanted to be the favorite of us. She cooked, helped Momma clean, and always sided with Poppa against Pete. She made her own clothes, and her skirts remained a conservative two inches above her knees.

Don't laugh, darling, but I wore miniskirts that showed my panties whenever I leaned over or sat down. We all did. Except Bareeba.

Looking back, I think Bareeba was terribly lonely. She had no friends her own age.

Once Bareeba caught me kissing a boy on the front lawn. It was a very innocent kiss. Bareeba screamed that I was a "tart bound for Hell!" She dragged Poppa and Momma out of the house to tell them about it. I was mortified. The boy fled. I hated Bareeba with every fiber of my sixteen-year-old body.

Now, however, I realize that the real problem was that nobody ever tried to kiss Bareeba. No boy would be caught dead even speaking to her. Then there was school. Good grades came easily to me. I rarely worked. Poor Bareeba struggled and struggled with school and managed with superhuman effort to maintain a B average.

The more I hated Bareeba, the more she hated me. She was always pointing out my faults to Poppa and whipping him up into one of his angry rages. The only person who stood up for me was Pete.

The Vietnam War was going full swing, and everywhere boys were being drafted to go and fight. Pete helped organize a protest in the town square.

His best friend ran away to Canada to avoid the draft. I told Pete he should run away, that I would run away with him, but he just laughed.

If anything, he was glad when his number finally came up. He said it was a chance to leave Green River.

I've always missed him. I never saw him again after that summer. I went sailing with the Crandalls, and he went off to Vietnam. Neither of us ever came back to Green River, Pennsylvania.

I'm a little tired now, darling. I think I'll rest before writing more.

> I love you with all my heart,
> Mom

P.S. Give Bartel Bear a pat on the head, and tell him to watch out for my little girl.

CHAPTER 3

Tommy rubbed her eyes with the back of her hand and carefully refolded the letter in its envelope. She put the letter neatly beside the photograph of her mother that stood on the bedside table.

That's the summer you met Jud, isn't it Mom? What did you see in him? Tommy sighed. What were you like then? Try as she might, Tommy could only picture her mother now, lying in bed, pale, trying to smile. She took the map from her bureau drawer and spread it out flat. With her finger, she traced and retraced the roads that led all the way from Bradenpond to Stapleton.

Every evening after dinner Jud would step outside to smoke a cigarette. Sometimes Tommy would watch him as he stared out at the night with his back to the house. He doesn't like this any more than I do, she thought bitterly. I guess we're stuck with each other.

After a week, Jud came back from his after-dinner cigarette and asked her to talk. Tommy shrugged her shoulders. She wasn't sure what they had to talk about, but she was very lonely, and even conversation with Jud was better than no conversation at all.

"You don't have to say yes," began Jud. It was an odd way to start a conversation. Tommy shoved her hands down hard in her pockets and squinted at him.

"What about?" she asked.

"Well, I been thinking about what Lida Barnaby said about it not being right—you just being here all the time."

"I don't mind." Except she did. Tommy minded terribly. She had no friends. She'd been able to get through to her mother only once on the telephone, and even then, Aunt Bareeba had let them talk for only five minutes. Then she had snatched the phone from her sister and said firmly to Tommy, "That's enough for now, Tamara. Your mother's tired and needs her rest."

"But Bareeba, I *want* to talk to my daughter," Tommy heard her mother protesting faintly in the background. "I love you, Mom," Tommy yelled into the telephone. But it was Bareeba who spoke. "You'll have to hang up now, Tamara. Your mother's a very sick woman."

Is she sicker than she was? Is she weaker? How much time does she have left? Tommy wanted to ask. But she knew that Bareeba wouldn't answer her questions. It was almost as if she didn't exist, or certainly as if Aunt Bareeba didn't *want* her to exist. Tommy felt shut off from her mother, as if Aunt Bareeba had built an impenetrable wall around her, and nobody but Aunt Bareeba was allowed in.

And I don't have any friends here, thought Tommy bitterly. I don't even know where I'll be going to school. I hate it. I hate this house. I hate Lida Barnaby, who ought to mind her own business.

"So anyway," Jud was speaking much longer than he usually did. "I asked Joe Bartlett—he kind of manages the boat yard—if he could do with some help in the office, and I said I had my daughter with me, for the summer at any rate, and since Cheryl Briggs ran off with that carpenter fellow from Bangor, he's a bit shorthanded. Well?"

"Well what?" asked Tommy who had been lost in her own thoughts.

"Do you want to work in the boat yard for the summer? I don't imagine it's hard. You just have to answer the phones and keep the records straight, that kind of thing. Won't pay much, about two-fifty an hour, and it's off the record, so you don't have to fool around with the damn IRS. Anyway, I got a feeling you're underage. I think you're supposed to be fourteen or some such nonsense. But Joe, he don't mind about that, long as you show up on time and do your work proper."

A lot of smelly old men like you? You must be kidding, thought Tommy. Maybe *I'm* the one who died and I've gone to Hell, only I don't know it's Hell, which really makes it only worse. She re-played the *Twilight Zone* music in her head, which she and Sheila Morton always used to do when they thought something was really weird. She tried her sweet smile—but left out the eye-batting part. "I don't think so, Jud. I don't know anything about boats. And I'd be way too young to fit in with your friends," she added diplomatically.

Jud rubbed his chin thoughtfully. "Well, you don't have to know about boats, you just answer the tele-phone. Some of the regulars are pretty close to your age. Of course, they go back to school in the fall. And sometimes the college fellas decide they want to work in a boat yard for the summer. And then of course there's the summer people with their boats. Just the other day, a boat came in with a girl on it about your age. She seemed kind of lonely. It made me think of you. Of course, they're gone now. Summer people never stay here long."

"I'm not lonely," snapped Tommy.

But, on second thought even Hell *might* be bearable with some boys in it. She shrugged her shoulders. "Sure," she said noncommittally. "Sure, I'll give it a try." Two-fifty an hour times eight and then five times that. Tommy knew she'd need a pencil to work out the math. But it would certainly supplement the "trip home money."

"Tomorrow then. You'll have to get up same as me at five. It's an hour to the yard. And I like to get there early."

"Okay."

But as Tommy lay in bed that night, she couldn't help but be excited by the prospect of working in the boat yard—actually getting out of the house and seeing new people. She set the alarm for four-thirty so that she could wash her hair and put on a little makeup. Jud had said jeans were fine. But there was no reason why she couldn't look nice in jeans.

I can't wait to tell Sheila about *this!* she thought to herself. She will be so jealous! All those cute young carpenters from college (!!!!) and splendid yachts with handsome captains. Summer People. Even the words had a magical ring to them. For the first time in several months, Tommy actually smiled as she drifted into sleep, writing an imaginary letter to Sheila all about her summer adventures.

Dear Sheila,

I have a real job. I work in a boat yard, and there are these really cute carpenters. . . . Well, one has blond hair and blue eyes and he's about six foot three, and he took me out in his speedboat and we went water-skiing . . . and then of course . . . Jamie, he's twenty-two and he has green eyes and black hair . . . he is really in love with me . . . but I'm not sure. Jud says he's a little old. . . . Then we went to a party in a huge mansion, and it turned out that Ted was actually an English lord, but he was just being a carpenter for the summer, and he . . .

Although maybe I'll be telling her in person. It shouldn't take me too long to save up enough.

A second later, or so it seemed, Tommy's alarm was clanging unbearably loudly in her ear. The room was pitch-black. "I can't believe I'm actually doing this," groaned Tommy as she swatted at the clock. All thoughts of yachts and cute boys had been replaced by a feeling of not enough sleep. "Wash hair," she moaned as she turned on the light and stumbled to the bathroom. The floor was cold under her bare feet. The water was even colder. It seemed to take hours to warm up. When it finally did, however, the shower playing on her body and face began to bring a little feeling of life back. She opened her mouth and tipped her head back to let the points of water dance and splash against her teeth. She liked the drumming hollow sound the water made as it hit her tongue and cheeks. The shampoo was soft and velvety in her hair.

Several minutes later, she emerged, much re-freshed, wrapped in her yellow terry cloth robe and scrubbing at her hair with her towel. Jud appeared at the foot of the stairs and looked up at her. "I was just coming to wake you," he said.

"Thanks, but I'm already up."

"I'll start the coffee."

It was still dark when Tommy came downstairs. She had put on a little makeup, and her hair was shiny and full from being blown dry. Self-con-sciously, she pushed her hands into her back pock-ets. But Jud was not paying any attention. He was involved in slathering Wonder bread with mayon-naise. The opened pack of bologna sat on the kitchen counter. "I usually make myself a sandwich for lunch," he said. "I made you one already, in that bag." He motioned with his head toward a brown paper bag. Tommy opened the bag and peered in. She saw a flat, white square encased in plastic wrap. Gross, she thought disgustedly. She could smell the greasy, sweet odor of prepackaged bologna emanating from the folds of Saran Wrap.

"Looks great, thanks," she cheerfully lied. "I think I'll take along an apple. I mean, I like to eat apples at lunch." How brilliant to have insisted on a bag of apples at the supermarket. At least she wouldn't starve.

"There's a soda machine there," Jud was saying.

"And Marie Smet drives a truck in around lunch break with sandwiches and things. But I don't buy from her. She charges a lot for what don't seem like much. You ready?"

"Sure. Are we going to eat breakfast?" asked Tommy a bit hesitantly.

"Well, I usually bring along coffee. I found those old Dundee marmalade jars keeps the heat in pretty good. Your mom liked that marmalade a lot, and the jars seemed kind of useful, so I kept them." His voice slowed down until it ground to a halt. Tommy wondered if she should say something, but before she could think of anything to say, Jud had resumed. "Then I usually stop at a Dunkin' Donuts at Elk's Corner. It's in the mall. I suppose you'll want to go to the mall someday we're not working. Lida says that's where the kids shop and hang around."

"No, that's okay," said Tommy abruptly. From now on, she was going to save every cent.

The sun was beginning to rise when they climbed into the old blue pickup. The dew was glimmering cold on the grass, and the truck was covered with tiny icy beads. Tommy hated the pickup. It made her feel poor and dirty. It made her think of phrases like "dirt farmer" and "trash." And it smelled! It reeked of dead fish and stale cigarettes. There were even some dried out lobster pots and nets behind the seats. Sheila Morton would die before she sat in a truck like this. What would the kids back home say if they knew? But home was far away. In this case, Tommy was thankful for the distance.

She hoped Jud wouldn't smoke, especially if it really did take an hour to get to "the yard." Jud handed her a mug (really a ceramic jar with the words "Dundee Marmalade") filled with coffee. She sniffed at the steam and felt the warmth of the jar seep into her fingers. She held the jar carefully as the pickup lurched and grumbled, backing out of the dirt driveway.

Jud drove with one hand and sipped his coffee with the other. When it was time to change gears, he rested his jar in his lap and then picked it up again.

Tommy nervously pushed her hair behind her ear and felt for her tiny diamond stud. "Jud, you sure it's okay if I work in the boat yard?"

"Yup. 'Course if you don't like it, you can quit."

Tommy shook her head. "I won't quit. I was just wondering. What's the name of the man who runs the boat yard?"

"Joe?"

"I guess so. Do I call him Joe?"

"Everyone else does. You don't have to call him Mr. Bartlett, if that was what you was wondering. You nervous?"

Tommy was about to shake her head "no," but found herself saying, "Yeah. A little, I guess."

Jud glanced at her, then put his coffee in his lap

and rather clumsily patted her shoulder. "I figured you were," he said gruffly, and then quickly withdrew his hand and took up his jar of coffee.

Embarrassed, Tommy looked out the window. "How far is it to the mall?" she asked.

" 'Bout another fifteen minutes or so. You hungry?"

Tommy nodded, although she wasn't really. The coffee was making her feel sick. It was strong, too strong for Tommy's liking, and she was glad that she had heaped in several teaspoons of Coffee-mate along with the splash of milk. Her stomach was cramping up from the caffeine by the time they reached the town of Elk's Corner. She tried not to wince. Well, the bright side was that if she had this much caffeine every morning, she'd be a midget in no time.

The pink tinges in the sky were giving way to blue now, and the pine trees and houses were clear in the morning light. Tommy found herself reading the street signs and looking at the dark windows. There was hardly anyone about.

The Elk's Corner Mall looked to Tommy as if it could be anywhere, even home. There was a large discount clothing store, a movie theater, a delicatessen, a Chinese restaurant, a hardware store, and a Dunkin' Donuts—the only establishment open at this hour, and of course the huge deserted parking lot. Tommy glanced at her watch. Six-ten read the dial. She groaned inwardly and wished she were still asleep.

The inside of the doughnut store was sparkling bright. Rows and rows of different kinds of doughnuts were displayed. A cheery young waitress with her hair slicked back in a hair net smiled when they came in. "Mornin', Jud," she called.

"Mornin', Ellen."

Ellen smiled at Tommy. "Brought your granddaughter along?" she asked.

"My daughter," answered Jud sharply.

"Didn't know you had a daughter." She laughed easily. "Got your favorite, apply jelly. Oh, good mornin', Mr. Sanders. I like your new truck."

Tommy pushed her hands into her pockets. She was feeling nauseated from the coffee and embarrassed by the waitress's remarks. "I think I'll have a corn muffin instead," she whispered to her father. The thought of apple jelly doughnuts was making her stomach feel clammy and sick. Jud nodded and quickly paid for the two items. He seemed almost to slam down the money on the counter, and when he left, he didn't say good-bye to Ellen.

They got into the truck in silence. Tommy hoped he wasn't annoyed with her for not having a doughnut.

Finally he spoke. "I'm sorry about what happened in there, Tommy."

Tommy shrugged her shoulders. "It's okay."

"That girl means well. I guess I never told her I had a daughter. I didn't think I looked old enough to have a granddaughter. I didn't use to look like this, you know. After your mother left, I kind of fell to pieces. There wasn't anything left. . . . And it's hard having you see me like this. I always hoped you'd never have to. . . ."

Tommy hesitated. "I thought maybe you were mad at me."

Jud turned to her. "Why?"

"I don't know. 'Cause I wanted a corn muffin instead of a doughnut, I guess."

"You can have whatever you want. I don't have any say in what you want," Jud snapped.

Tommy shrugged her shoulders. She could feel her eyes stinging. What am I doing here? she asked silently. Why did Mom have to be sick? She could almost feel her mother gently brushing back the wisp of hair that always fell into her eyes. And that little half smile that her mother had.

I can't think about her, thought Tommy. I might start to cry. And Jud will *never* see me cry. She bit her lip hard. I hate it here, she screamed inside her head. I hate everything about Maine. I hate my father and he hates me. And I'm going home just as soon as I have enough money.

Being angry helped. The prickly feeling behind

her eyes receded. She tossed her head and looked out the window.

"I'm sorry, Tommy," Jud said quietly. "I'm kind of mad at Ellen, though she's a nice girl and means well. . . . You look like your mother a lot," he added thoughtfully.

Tommy faced Jud. "Yeah," she answered. "That's what everyone says." I'll bet that's why we don't get along, she thought to herself. I look just like Mom, and Mom left him. Well I don't blame her for that. I can't see why she married him in the first place.

The road ran close to the shore now. Tommy could see the expanses of twinkling blue water beyond the trees and stony fields. A woman was hanging out wash. The sheets flapped and curled as she clipped them to the line. Her mouth was full of clothespins. She managed to wave at Jud's pickup as they passed. He lifted his hand and nodded in response. "That's Mary Bartlett, Joe's wife. Sometimes she makes things for the men at the yard to eat, 'specially 'round the holidays. And come Thanksgiving and Christmas we have a turkey raffle. Biggest damn birds you ever saw. I never won, though."

Jud turned the truck into a dirt driveway, full of potholes. Ahead, Tommy could see several large wooden structures, all a weathered gray; beyond, water glistened in the sunlight. There were several other cars and trucks in the parking lot. As Jud picked up the lunch bags and slammed the door shut on the pickup, a tall man with a blue cap on his head and heavy navy overalls came out of one of the buildings. Jud waved to him. "Mornin', Matt," he called. "I want you to meet my daughter. Her name's Tommy, and she's stayin' with me for the summer."

"Well, I'll be," said the tall man, and he wiped his hands on his canvas overalls before coming over. "Well, I'll be. Ain't she a picture though? A real picture. Hey, Judge, a real surprise, your having a daughter."

"I'm a surprise to everyone," quipped Tommy.

The boat yard proved different from what Tommy had imagined. The three outbuildings where boats were stored over the winter were huge and dirty. They looked like misshapen barns. The paint was peeling on the outside, and the few windows were cracked or missing panes entirely.

A work room behind the front office was filled with power tools and huge tables. Overhead, long strips of fluorescent bulbs flickered. The floor was black with dirt, and the corners were filled with sawdust.

Between the buildings, crabgrass and dandelions struggled to grow in the pebbly earth. The place was littered with cigarette butts, bottle caps, and the occasional shard of broken glass. It was uglier and poorer than Tommy had expected. She was quite ready to hate it . . . until she saw the harbor.

She stood silently on the ramp that led down to the dock. She felt almost dizzy. It was so painfully beautiful.

Was it possible that water and sky could be such an intense blue? The colors of the shore so luxuriously vibrant? The pink and white granite boulders, the black seaweed, the glistening pearly barnacles—farther out, the boats, neatly spaced, clean and perfect. Tommy let the cool morning breeze play on her face. She closed her eyes and listened to the raucous cry of sea gulls, the sound of a motor starting, and the whispering of the seaweed as it drifted up and down on smooth swells.

She didn't mind when she sensed Jud standing beside her.

"It's kind of pretty," he said slowly.

She nodded. "It's just that I've never seen the sea before," she said truthfully. For a while, the two of them stood shoulder to shoulder and looked out over the harbor.

Jud broke the silence. "Well," he said, "now that you've seen the water, Joe wants you to see the inside of the office."

Reluctantly, Tommy walked back. A string of bells jingled as she pushed open the office door. Joe Bartlett sprang to his feet. He was an enormous man, wearing a huge gray sweatshirt. "Good to meet you, Tommy," he bellowed in a cheerful voice. "Didn't get her looks from you, Judge, that's for sure. You'll add some sparkle 'round this place. . . . Hey," his voice became conspiratorial, "you don't mind the calendar, do you?"

Hanging directly over the desk was a 1955 calendar displaying an extremely well-endowed blond female wearing nothing but a cheerleading skirt, climbing out of a red car. Tommy couldn't help but glance ruefully down at her own T-shirt, plastered flat against her chest.

"See your dad here, he wanted to take it down, on account of you working here. Said it wasn't proper. But it's been on the wall as long as I can remember. Hell, the wall might fall down. It's that much a part of the place, and I thought I'd ask you first."

Embarrassed, Tommy shrugged her shoulders. "I don't mind."

"You see, Judge, she doesn't mind," laughed Joe in an easygoing way. "But you know, Judge, if I had a daughter, I'd be just the same. Yep, just the same," he added kindly.

As the morning progressed, Tommy found herself liking Joe. He laughed a lot and made silly jokes as he showed her around the office.

After what seemed like only ten minutes, Joe announced that it was coffee break time. Suddenly the small room was filled with men smelling of turpentine and sweat lining up at the coffee machine. Joe waved a paper cup at her invitingly, but she shook her head. She didn't feel like talking, and she really didn't feel like drinking any more coffee.

Taking an old legal pad and a ballpoint pen, she wandered out to the wharf and settled down to share her first day of work.

Dear Mom,

Guess what? I got a job today. A real job! Not a baby-sitting job! I'm working in the boat yard with Jud. I make $2.50 an hour! I'd make more if I was a carpenter or a painter. But I'm working in the office. I have to answer the telephone, saying, "Four Bays Boat Yard. This is Tommy speaking. Can I help you?" And then everybody thinks I'm a boy. So I have to tell them I'm a girl. But I guess it doesn't matter, except it does to me. Joe, he's the manager, is going to teach me how to keep track of the launch charges. But I think that will take some time. It seems pretty complicated.

I think the boat yard fixes mostly lobster boats and fishing boats. But we do have a few big boats that belong to summer people.

Love,
Tommy

CHAPTER
4

"Now, this is the record of launch charges, and this is the gas, and the electric hookup at the dock. Repairs would be listed here." Joe had opened several books and arranged them in front of Tommy. She frowned as she forced herself to study the columns of figures and squiggles of notations. This was worse than school.

"Don't worry about understanding the bookkeeping right away. It takes some time. Just ask me if you don't know what to write down." Joe's voice was kind. Tommy nodded gratefully.

The door to the office opened and shut with a bang. Several papers on the desk jumped in the draft. Impatiently, Tommy slapped her hand down on them.

"Excuse me, Joe. There's something wrong with the starter motor on the launch, and Mrs. Phillips wants to get out to the *February*."

"Yeah, yeah. Can't you see I'm busy? Just row her out, Chris. You don't need the launch. And this is Tommy. She's taking Cheryl's place. *February fourteenth*, what a stupid name for a boat."

"Must have been a Valentine's Day present," volunteered Tommy. Then she blushed. What a ridiculous thing to say. She looked up and saw a boy, not much older than herself, standing, looking at her. Well, he certainly wasn't anything like the fantasies that she had written about in her imaginary letter. He had a black grease smear on his cheek and a lot of freckles on his nose. He was skinny with large dirty "boy" hands coming out of his sleeves.

"Hi, Tommy," he said. "I guess you're new here."

"Yeah, you guessed right," she answered, unimpressed.

Joe laughed. "Okay, you've met the new girl, Chris. Now, run along and row Mrs. Phillips to her boat if you can't get the launch running. You can talk to Tommy at lunch break."

"Fat chance," muttered Tommy as she stacked the papers on the desk. It was so embarrassing to have this boy try and pick her up right in front of Joe (as well as underneath that awful calendar). And besides, he definitely was not her type. Peter Farber, where are you? she asked inside her head.

Back home in Stapleton, stupid, she answered herself sourly.

By the end of the day, she was exhausted. She slept the one hour drive back to the house and was almost too tired to eat the hamburgers that Jud brought in from McDonald's.

After dinner, she flopped down on her bed to read the letter that had arrived while she was at work.

My darling Tommy,

That was the summer that changed my life. I was seventeen. I had spent all my life in Green River, sharing a room with Bareeba that was painted an awful canary yellow. Except that by that summer, the paint had faded and cracked. The color underneath was a dark green. It always felt like Bareeba's room. It seemed as if the only person who cared about me was Pete.

Momma loved Bareeba. She kept telling me I should be more like her. Poppa was always yelling at me. Pete said I was Poppa's favorite, but at the time it didn't seem so.

I vowed when you were born that I would never make you feel the way my parents made me feel. I've always wanted you to feel loved and cared for. Because you are. You're the most important thing in the world to me. And one reason I feel so darn

ANGRY about this sickness is that I won't be able to watch you grow up and help you the way a mother is supposed to.

Anyway, back to that summer. Uncle George and Aunt Sissy invited me to go sailing with them up from Maryland along the coast to Maine. Then to stay for the summer in Wink's Cove. The closest town is Blue Hill, which is tiny in itself. So that gives you an idea of Wink's Cove. Nevertheless, Wink's Cove takes itself very seriously—or at least the summer people do. It has a yacht club and a country club and a general store.

Uncle George and Aunt Sissy were not really my aunt and uncle. Although I think Uncle George was distantly related to Poppa.

To this day, I wonder what prompted him to include me. Either it was an act of charity for a poor relation, or else they wanted me as a companion for their daughter, Louisa, who was my age. They did not invite Bareeba, which made her very angry. I felt terrific because finally I was doing something on my own.

Momma said she would make it up to Bareeba by buying her a car. That somewhat dampened my enthusiasm.

I bought my first diary that summer. I have it in front of me now. It's pink with rosebuds in the four corners, and it has a lock. I didn't want Bareeba snooping.

I spent many hours that spring, daydreaming about

huge yachts cutting through icy blue waters, white sails, and the wind in my hair.

Tommy smiled as she thought of the huge sailing boats moored in the harbor of the boat yard—sleek and polished with teak decks and tight rigging and neatly furled sails. They seemed almost like thoroughbred horses pulling back against their tethers. Mooring lines, straight and taut. There was something about the waves and the sea birds that made you want to daydream—as if you could fly up into the cold air on wings like sails and swoop down to skim the foam from the water's surface.

Jud knocked on the door. Tommy quickly folded the letter and put it in its envelope. "It's okay, Jud," she said. "Come in."

"I just came up to say good night. I wanted to make sure you were all right. I figured you weren't used to getting up so early."

"I'm fine, Jud. I was just going to turn in."

Jud nodded. "Well . . . sleep well, Tommy. I just wanted to tell you, you did real good on your first day at work. Joe and everyone like you a lot. . . . So, anyway, good night."

Jud withdrew, closing the door gently behind him. Tommy poked her hair thoughtfully behind her ear and sat cross-legged on her bed for a moment. Maybe

Jud wasn't all *that* bad after all. He just took some getting used to.

Even though she turned out her light at eight-thirty, she had to force her eyes open when her alarm rang in her ear at four-thirty A.M. "I am definitely not a morning person," she mumbled as she staggered into the bathroom to wash her hair. Jud's coffee helped some, and by the time they reached the boat yard, Tommy had somewhat woken up.

"*Taffey's Dawn*, she'll be leaving tomorrow," explained Joe, as he pointed out a large sloop with a green hull. Tommy could see a woman sunbathing on the deck. The woman sat up, shaded her sunglasses as she looked toward shore, and lay back down again. "Ain't that the life, though," said Joe admiringly. "Well, come on back to the office, I'll show you the records. They said they'd be off first thing in the morning. 'Course that means eight o'clock at the earliest. Ain't that the life?"

"Yeah," answered Tommy wistfully. She had never been sailing in her life, but she could imagine it so clearly that it almost hurt. . . . To sail away on a beautiful boat with clean salty wind blowing your hair back, and the sound and feel of waves slapping the bottom of the boat as the huge sails pulled you forward, cutting through the foam . . . To watch the shoreline slide past . . . Or to lie in the sun as

the boat rocked . . . your back all warm . . . and
when you breathed, the smell of the sea mixed with
the sweet smell of suntan oil . . . And never to have
to worry about anything . . . ever.

At lunch break, Tommy stayed close to Jud. They
ate their sandwiches sitting on some huge beams
that were stacked in one corner of the open space
between the buildings. A mangy German shepherd
ambled over to beg for food. He wagged his tail and
looked longingly at Tommy's sandwich. Tommy
obliged and gave him most of the bologna. After he
gulped it down, he nuzzled his nose under her hand
for a pat. "Hello, dog," she said gently.

"His name's Buddy," informed Jud. "He hangs out
here and guards the place at night. Guess you could
say he belongs to Joe, but Mary won't have him in
the house. Can't say I blame her."

"I have a dog at home," volunteered Tommy slowly.
"Dozer. But Aunt Bareeba put him in a kennel."

Jud looked at her for a moment. "I didn't know
you had a dog," he said thoughtfully. "Well, eat your
apple. You gave all your sandwich to that mutt. I
don't want your mother saying I starve you."

After work, Tommy made spaghetti and salad for
dinner. She wasn't quite as tired as the night before,
and besides, spaghetti was easy, almost automatic.
She'd cooked a lot of spaghetti dinners back home
when she was taking care of her mother.

After dinner, Jud separated out a letter for Tommy that had gotten mixed in with an A&P circular. He went outside for his cigarette, and Tommy took the letter to her room.

Uncle George's boat was called *The Little Princess.* He called Louisa "Princess." I never knew whether he named the boat after his daughter, or his daughter after the boat.

Poor Louisa. She had a terrible complexion problem—one of the worst I've ever seen. She spent most of the time picking at her face. Sometimes she would read in a deck chair wearing a huge white floppy hat.

Aunt Sissy seemed to almost despise her own daughter. Aunt Sissy was very beautiful in a cold, blond way. She always wore very tight white jeans and dark sunglasses. And she NAGGED and CRITICIZED. I can still hear her raspy voice (she was a chain-smoker and her voice was husky and thick): "Louisa, look at Elaine. Elaine doesn't eat chocolate. Do you, dear? And Elaine exercises. Elaine dear, you have a beautiful figure. And what a lovely tan Elaine is getting."

"The doctor said not to get my zits sunburned, okay?" Louisa would snarl.

"Well, surely, dear, he didn't mean for you to spend the entire summer white as a ghost. And we don't use the word "zits." Blemishes is so much more—how do you say it? Elaine, help me with this one—

refined. Ladylike. Louisa, you do understand what I'm talking about, don't you? And please refrain from slumping. Shoulders back, darling. Tummy in. That hat really is hideous."

Then of course, Uncle George. He was the type of man who liked to shout orders. He made us all wear specially designed T-shirts. His said admiral, Aunt Sissy's said first mate, and mine and Louisa's said crew.

Uncle George worshiped Louisa. To him, she was the most beautiful, perfect being in the world. He had a horrible habit of saying out of the clear blue, "My princess is the prettiest girl in the world, and all the guys are in love with her." Then he would say to Louisa, "You tell your mother I'm right." He never spoke directly to Aunt Sissy unless he absolutely had to. He used Louisa to speak for him as much as possible.

The person who did the most work was Captain Hank. He was very careful to always salute Uncle George and would make a show of consulting him on all aspects of the journey, but he was the one who really kept the boat on course.

That cruise up the east coast was a combination of torture (I found myself hating the entire family) and a dream. July third, I wrote in my diary: "I think I am falling in love. Not with a boy . . . with the sea. It's so blue and clean. Yesterday, I saw baby seals sliding off seaweed-covered rocks in the middle of the harbor. They were all fat and golden with soft shaggy fur. Sometimes grown-up seals poke their noses out of the water if they think you have a fish for them. They are black and shiny with long whiskers and beady eyes. When I look at the seals and the blue, blue water and the way even the sky seems clean and pure, I don't think I ever want to live away from the ocean. Part of me will always be here. . . ."

Dear Mom,

I've only just started work, and I know what you mean about the sea. Beyond the boat yard, there's a craggy shore made up of huge granite boulders. I can see the waves breaking and how the water sparkles in the sun. I feel very far away from Stapleton. I guess I'm feeling a little bit the way you felt.

I love you, Mom.
Tommy xxxxooooo

And Mom—There's a dog at the yard. I shared my lunch with him. It made me think of Dozer. I really miss him. I miss you more, of course. But I keep remembering how Dozer howled when the man at the kennel took him away, and how he kept dragging at his leash trying to get back to us. Jud said I could pat Buddy anytime I wanted. But it's not the same. Besides, I think Buddy has fleas.

Anyway, I'm pretty tired. Believe it or not, I have to get up at 5:00, and if I want to wash my hair, it had better be earlier. Was your hair *really* like mine when you were my age—all thin and greasy, unless it's washed every day? I can't imagine you with thin hair. But you were never tall. I think I got your hair and Aunt Bareeba's size. What a frightening thought. At least I'm not fat.

I love you always and always.
Tommy

P.S. It's hard to imagine you young. It's *impossible* to imagine Bareeba young.

By the end of the week, Tommy had gotten used to the routine. She'd even gotten used to Jud's coffee. She found she spent less time studying her map and counting her money for her escape. Probably because I'm so tired from work, she rationalized to herself.

Dearest Tommy,

I'm so proud of you getting a real job. I want you to know I'm doing just fine. I'm even feeling a little better, which is a great surprise to everyone, especially the doctor and Aunt Bareeba.

Now, darling, you may have inherited your hair from me, but there's a lot of Jud in you too. He was a very handsome young man, tall and not fat in the least. I would imagine that you favor him in the height department, not your Aunt Bareeba.

I never told you much about him.

I was only seventeen. . . . It seems so long ago, and yet if I close my eyes, the years seem to vanish and I'm there again. . . .

I first saw Jud when *The Little Princess* pulled into Blue Hill. Actually, got stuck is more like it. Uncle George insisted on taking the helm and promptly ran us aground so that the launch had to come and tow us out. Apparently this happened every year. Uncle George could never figure out how to maneuver through the black can and red nun that marked the safe course.

"Jud," called Tommy down the stairs. "Jud, what's a black can and a red nun? I know it has something to do with sailing."

"Markers. Shows you where the channels are."

Tommy sat with her knees tucked under her chin halfway down the stairs. "And?" she persisted.

Jud stood outside his room, his hand resting on the banister, and looked up at her. "See, sometimes, coming into the harbor, there might be rocks and shallow places that you can't see."

"Yeah, but what do they look like? I mean a 'red nun'?" The image of a crimson Virgin Mary statue, hands outstretched, standing on a rock in the middle of the ocean, was all she could think of, and somehow that didn't seem right.

Jud frowned and rubbed his chin. "Well," he said

slowly. "A black can looks sort of like a black can on a stick. And the nun looks sort of like a red cone. I'll show you at the yard tomorrow, if you like." He turned away from Tommy as if thinking hard. "You can always remember how to do it, if you think *Red, Right, Returning*. When you're coming back into the harbor, you pass the red nun on your right, and the black can on your left. That way you're always safe." Jud's voice had changed somehow, becoming clearer as he explained the terms to Tommy. It seemed, however, that he wasn't speaking to her but to someone else. "Always safe," he repeated slowly.

"You okay, Jud?" called Tommy. It seemed that Jud spent a lot of time staring into space.

He turned slowly and looked up at her. His eyes were tired and sad. He nodded. "Yup. You wanted to ask me something?"

"You answered me already," called Tommy, and she scrambled back up to her room, impatient to finish the precious letter.

Anyway, out from the harbor ploughed this old launch, and as it approached, I could see a tall, blond man at the wheel. He waved cheerfully at Uncle George and said something like, "Afternoon, Mr. Crandall. Guess it's that time of year again."

"Jud, you're always moving those damn markers all over creation. I don't know how anybody gets in or out of here without going aground. Isn't that so, Captain Hank? You said they moved the markers, didn't you, Captain Hank?"

Poor Captain Hank muttered something unintelligible and came as close to blushing as a man can. But I wasn't interested in Captain Hank. . . . I was watching Jud—who was the most handsome man I had ever seen. He saw me staring, gave a wink and a grin, and then concentrated on tying the lines that were thrown back and forth between the two boats.

"He's a local," said Louisa with a sniff. I didn't know what she meant. I felt the most wonderful thrill wash over me, and I reveled in this new feeling. His name is Jud, I thought to myself. Then I said his name several times over inside my head, so that I wouldn't *ever* forget it.

And that's how it began.

I love you, darling. Hugs and kisses. xxxxooooo
Mom

Sunday, the boat yard was closed. Jud said he had an errand to do and drove off in the pickup. Tommy was left alone to amuse herself. The housework had piled up, so she spent most of the morning vacuuming and scrubbing. Finally, the kitchen and bathroom were decent. Jud's house was beginning to look halfway normal.

Lida Barnaby dropped by and complimented

Tommy on the tidiness of the kitchen, which made Tommy feel a combination of pride (which was encouraging) and Suzie Homemaker (which was definitely discouraging).

"Met anyone your own age, dear?" asked Mrs. Barnaby, as she leaned back with a sigh. She had accepted and drunk the cup of tea that Tommy offered.

"No."

"Well, now, dear, you really should go to church. Lots of fine young men go to church, with their families, of course, and it's a good way to meet people. Besides, church is an important part of life."

Tommy frowned. "My mom doesn't go to church. Not everybody does."

Lida Barnaby's expression was one of shocked disapproval. "Don't you believe in the Almighty?" she asked reproachfully.

Dear Mom,

Lida Barnaby dropped by today and wanted to know if I believe in God. I said yes, but I'm not sure if I do. I certainly don't believe in a God who allowed you to get cancer. And even if He exists, I'm not going to pray to Him.

Besides, you and I never went to church. Jud doesn't go to church. He's off on some errand. Of course I don't know where he's gone or when he'll be back.

It's Sunday, and I have nothing to do. I even cleaned the house this morning—including the toilet! I really think I'd make a good cleaning lady.

Only joking. I guess I'm in a bad mood because it seems like Lida Barnaby is always prying or bossing. Don't worry, Mom. I'm very polite. But upstairs, I hear Bartel Bear growl whenever she comes. He doesn't like her.

But he does like Jud. I like Jud too, at least most of the time.

But Mom, I don't love him. I don't really feel like he's my father. However, since I never really had a father that I can remember (Allen certainly doesn't count), maybe I just don't know what it feels like to have a father.

Anyway, I do know what it feels like to have a mother. I really need you, Mom. Please have it be true that you are getting better. I miss you, and I want to come home.

I love you,
Tommy

CHAPTER
5

It was nearly seven when Tommy heard the pickup in the driveway. Frowning, she looked out the window. There was nothing salvageable for dinner, and by now the King Kullen in Bradenpond proper would be closed, unless they drove all the way to the mall, where the A&P stayed open until nine o'clock on Sunday nights.

Jud was slow getting out of the truck. He seemed to be having trouble shutting the door. Tommy suddenly had a terrible thought that maybe he was sick. "You okay, Jud?" she called anxiously.

"Yeah, I'm fine," he yelled back cheerfully. "Why don't you come here though?"

As Tommy walked uncertainly toward the truck,

Jud opened the door to let a large brown wiggling body leap through the air.

"Dozer!" cried Tommy in disbelief. Dozer hurtled himself to Tommy, barking, whining, licking, and even half howling in his eagerness. Finally, Tommy was able to disentangle herself. "How did you get him?" she asked.

Jud grinned and ran his hand through his hair. "Well, when you said you had a dog but Bareeba had put him in a kennel, I thought you might like to have him here, so I had him shipped. His crate's in the back of the truck. But I felt kind of sorry for him because he was howling up a storm, so I let him sit with me in the front. We kind of got to know each other a bit," he added.

"Oh, Jud, thank you, thank you, thank you!" Tommy almost felt as if she wanted to wrap her arms around Jud's neck, she felt so happy, but she found herself patting Dozer instead. "Dozer, I missed you so much!" All of a sudden, Tommy was crying. Dozer tried to lick her face with his wet pink tongue. She tried to keep her head down, so that Jud wouldn't notice. But he put his hand on her shoulder. "I know," he said gently. "You've had a pretty hard time, haven't you?"

Tommy nodded and looked up to see an earnest worried look in Jud's eyes. He must think I'm a real jerk—crying like this, she thought to herself. She wiped her eyes with the back of her sleeve. "I'm okay now, Jud," she said. "I was just so surprised, that's all."

"I guess we'll have to make a run to the mall tonight and get some dog food," Jud said, as he hefted the shipping crate out of the back of the truck.

Tommy stood up and shoved her hands into her pockets. "Among other things," she said. "We have no apples, no lettuce, no eggs. We need another loaf of bread."

Jud nodded and glanced at his watch. "Better do it now," he said. Tommy climbed in the truck. "Well, come on, Dozer," said Jud patting the seat. Dozer flew into the truck and wiggled his large sleek body between Jud and Tommy. "I figured he'd be unhappy if we left him behind," mumbled Jud apologetically as the dog licked Tommy's ear and tried to crawl into her lap.

Two hours later, Jud and Tommy hefted paper bag after paper bag from the back of the pickup, up the porch steps, through the screen door, and into the kitchen—Dozer eagerly accompanying each trip and getting underfoot as much as caninely possible.

Tommy had stocked up on yogurt—raspberry, cherry, strawberry, and blueberry. "Joe said I could use the fridge in the office if I wanted," she explained.

Jud gave one of his rare grins. "Guess you're not too keen on my bologna sandwiches," he said.

"Oh, it's not that," began Tommy. Then she saw by the grin that it would be okay to be honest. "Well, I don't really like bologna," she admitted.

"I figured as much," said Jud. Then he gave a low laugh. He seemed younger when he laughed. Tommy found she was laughing too.

P.S. The reason Jud was gone today was because he went to pick up Dozer at the airport. It was a real surprise. Dozer likes Jud a lot. He keeps pushing his nose under Jud's hand for a pat. Jud says he's a pretty smart dog. It's still hard for me to think of Jud as MY FATHER, but I'm sort of starting to like him as a person. He doesn't seem quite so old now.

> I love you,
> Tommy

Jud gently kneed Dozer back into the house, while he balanced the two jars of coffee. "No, fella, you got to stay here. Joe don't want dogs in the yard."

Tommy winced as the truck pulled out of the driveway. She could see Dozer's head as he stood on his hind legs, with his nose pressed against the glass window in the door.

It was Monday, and another week was beginning at the yard. Tommy had started calling it the yard. She still had trouble with the flat stretched out "ah" sound, but she had the intonation down pretty good. "Jud? You think Dozer'll be okay?"

Jud sipped slowly from his marmalade jar. "Ayuh. He's a smart dog. He'll probably lay down and go to sleep on the sofa."

"You don't mind?" asked Tommy cautiously.

"Does he have fleas?"

"No, of course not."

"Then I don't mind. As long as he gets off when I want to sit there myself."

"Oh." This was a new turn of events. Even Mom had objections to Dozer napping on the furniture. Aunt Bareeba was a maniac on the subject. Tommy suppressed a giggle as she remembered Aunt Bareeba waddling angrily after Dozer with a spray can of Lysol in one hand and a rolled up newspaper in the other.

"Well?" asked Jud as he glanced at her over his coffee.

Tommy laughed out loud. "I was thinking of Aunt Bareeba chasing poor Dozer and trying to disinfect him with Lysol. And if she couldn't do that, she was going to swat 'the devil out of him' with a rolled up newspaper."

"Sounds like Bareeba," agreed Jud. "I guess she hasn't changed much."

"She's fatter," answered Tommy.

"Guess she still thinks I'm no good," said Jud thoughtfully.

Tommy looked down at her coffee. She felt uneasy at the sudden turn in the conversation. "I don't know," she lied. "Aunt Bareeba never said anything about you one way or the other."

Jud eyed Tommy as if he was going to say something but changed his mind. He stared ahead at the road. Tommy stared out the window at the shuttered houses of the approaching town of Elk's Corner. Her coffee had gone cold, and her mouth tasted flat.

Darling Tommy,

Maine really *is* beautiful. I remember so many things now that I thought I had forgotten or filed away as not important.

Uncle George and Aunt Sissy rented a huge old house on Tippling Boot Point, a squashy boot-shaped peninsula that jutted out into the bay and comprised most of Wink's Cove. The Boot, as it was called, was a compound of twenty or so "summer houses"— huge old shingled mansions—all in varying stages of decay. The families who "summered" there had been doing so for years—if not generations.

I had a tiny room of my own on the third floor. Louisa had claimed the second-floor bedroom, which was quite large and had new wallpaper and a big double closet. But her view was of the woods and the driveway that led to another house.

My window overlooked the bay. Louisa remarked that my room was technically a maid's room, but since they had day help, it was never used. She knew the house well. They had rented it every summer that she could remember.

I loved my room, with its old-fashioned wallpaper and white lace curtains. I could see the boats in the harbor, the blue, blue water, the gulls flying, and the stars in the black night sky.

I even had my own tiny bathroom with a funny square tub that you had to pull your knees up to your chin to fit in. There was a shower with it, but the water ran either very hot or very cold. Back in Green River, however, I was used to sharing a bathroom with four other people. A bathroom to myself was pure luxury.

No, I wouldn't have traded my room with Louisa's for anything!

The day after we arrived, Uncle George drove us over to the Yacht Club for sailing races. We stood around on the dock, and Louisa introduced me to her friends. "This is my parents' houseguest. Her name is Elaine."

They eyed me with cold interest. "Do you sail?" asked a rather plump boy with freckles. I shook my head. The boy shrugged his shoulders and asked Louisa how the trip up had been, to which she replied, "God-awful," and gave me a glance, which I interpreted to mean that she held me personally responsible. I looked out over the dock to the moored boats. I saw Jud tinkering with an outboard that wouldn't start. He didn't see me.

The races were scheduled for the afternoon. I

learned this was the *first* race of the season, which made it an important event. Soon Louisa and her friends were heading off to various boats to get them rigged before the race began. There was great activity and confusion as they hefted huge canvas sail bags on their shoulders and tramped down the ramp to the dock.

"I've already got my crew," said Louisa to me. "You don't mind, do you? Besides, you don't even know how to sail."

"That's okay." I tried to sound as if I didn't care. But I did. Uncle George wasn't going to return until the end of the afternoon. I was all alone in a strange place. How would I spend the afternoon?

I stood for a while on the dock and watched the boats being rigged. One by one, I saw the mainsails being hoisted up, rattling in the breeze. One by one, I saw the buoys being dropped from the boats and each boat give a sudden swing to catch the wind and begin zigzagging up to the mouth of the harbor.

"Not sailing today?" I heard a voice ask. It was Jud. I shook my head. "Why don't you go with Louisa? She's got room for one more. I can drop you off before the race starts."

"I'd just be in the way. I don't know how to sail," I explained nervously. "I thought you worked in Blue Hill," I added.

Jud grinned. "Only when somebody runs aground and needs a tow. Don't know how to sail? We'll have to do something about that," he said. "But in the meantime, it's pretty boring sitting here all afternoon. Why don't you come on the Committee Boat and watch the race?"

So I got to watch the race from the launch. It was quite exciting, at least the start and the finish. Jud fired off the cannon several times, and different colored flags were whipped up and down the flagpole.

After the race started, there wasn't much to do except wait for the boats to go around their course.

"Heard the *Princess* came in last night and got stuck again. Crandall's a real—"

Jud shot a warning look at the speaker, a pockmarked boy with glasses and greasy hair. Then he tipped his head in my direction.

"It's okay," I said quickly. "It's not like Uncle George is my *real* uncle. I mean he is related to my father but only distantly."

A boy with long blond hair tied back in a low ponytail asked me what my father did. "He's retired," I answered. There was no way I was going to say that my father was an electrician who moonlighted as a plumber in his spare time.

Quad, that was the boy's nickname, said he wished his father would retire. I later learned his father was head of a major law firm in New York City who wanted his son to study law and eventually take over the firm. Quad's father was in his sixties.

All Quad wanted to do was "hang out" and maybe go to California where a lot of his friends had "like, bought this farm." I said I had friends who had done that. A lie. I didn't know anyone in California.

Perhaps I should have told the truth. But I didn't. I was embarrassed by where I came from . . . and I didn't want Jud to think less of me. Besides, if I kept my mouth shut and learned to sail, *maybe* I would fit in.

When Tommy and Jud returned from work, there was a note pinned to the door.

Shut the damn dog up, or I'm calling the sheriff.

Dozer was ecstatic to see them. He leapt, whined, barked, and jumped. Tommy quickly let him out as they had been gone since 5:30 that morning. But he refused to "do anything" until she walked beside him on the scruffy lawn.

Inside, it became instantly clear that he had gotten into the garbage. It was strewn and chewed all over the kitchen, and an egg carton and an empty bologna package had been dragged into the living room. Jud shook his head and sighed.

"Dozer, how could you?" scolded Tommy frantically. She felt like crying. Now Jud would send Dozer back. Not only was some irate neighbor going to call the sheriff, but there was garbage all over everywhere. Dozer whined, flattened himself, and crept abjectly into a corner, the end of his tail quivering with emotion.

Tommy quickly picked up the chewed items and stuffed them back into the garbage pail. "It's okay, Jud. I've got it cleaned up. Dozer must have been scared or something. He's not like this usually. I promise."

Jud lit a cigarette and frowned. "It's not the mess, Tommy. I'm just worried about Clyde Cormer. I don't want trouble with the sheriff."

"It won't happen again, Jud. I promise. Dozer won't bark. He'll be really quiet."

Jud inhaled thoughtfully. "Well, I don't know, Tommy. I don't know. I can't have trouble."

Dear Mom,

I am so worried I don't know what to do. We left Dozer at the house while we went to work and he destroyed the place! He dragged garbage all over the living room, and he barked—bad enough for someone to tack a note on the door saying they were going to call the sheriff.

I was so happy to have Dozer with me. It was like home and you and the way things used to be. And now I'm afraid I'm going to lose him again.

I feel that no matter how hard I try, I'm losing everything! Everything! And sometimes at night, I think the most stupid thoughts. Like what if Peter

Farber decides he likes Sheila Morton better than me? Then I've lost him too. I don't have any friends here. What will school be like?

I know sometimes in the past you and I did fight. I shouldn't have bought that black tube top when you didn't approve. I'm really sorry. And I'm also sorry for anything I said that hurt your feelings. And the times when I lost my temper about stupid things— like what we were having for dinner, or me staying out too late. I know I lied a few times too, about where I was going, and then I covered it up, and yelled at you for not trusting me when you got suspicious. I'll never lie to you again. I promise. I'll do everything you ask. And you'll only have to ask once.

Please let me come home. I'll be really good. I'll take care of you, I promise. I'll never complain about anything. Just please let me come home where I belong. Please!!!

I love you.
Tommy

Dozer stayed close to Tommy that evening. He seemed to know that he had done wrong by the way he kept rolling his brown eyes up to meet hers, and fluttering the tip of his tail nervously, as if to say, "You still love me, don't you?"

Tommy felt too sick to eat any dinner and left for her room, saying she had a headache. Jud frowned

and shook his head in a way that Tommy knew meant:
We can't keep the dog anymore. "I'll call Clyde and
tell him to keep his shirt on until I figure things out,"
was all he said.

"I'm really sorry, Jud, about the mess and the
barking." Tommy went slowly up the stairs. It was
no use saying Dozer wouldn't do it again. Who
knew what Dozer would do? He was in a strange
house, left alone for hours, with a tempting garbage
pail, and strange cars and people passing outside.
He probably would bark while they were gone. And
he probably *would* get into the garbage. He wasn't
the most brilliant dog to begin with and certainly
not the most obedient. "But he's mine," whispered
Tommy fiercely. "He's all I've got!"

She took out her map and recounted her money.
But now with Dozer . . . How could she get Dozer
on a Greyhound bus?

My darling Tommy,

Please don't worry about our ups and downs. You
are the best daughter anyone could ever have. Part
of growing up is fighting with your parents about
clothes and curfews and allowances. Yes, it hurts me
when we fight. Sometimes we both say things that
we shouldn't. We end up hurting each other. But
darling, that's normal.

Tommy, spending this time with Jud is *not* a punishment. There is nothing to punish you for. You are a perfect daughter, and I thank God every day for you being a part of my life.

It's face-facts time (something I've never been very good at). Sooner or later, you will be living with Jud. He's a good man, and if you give him a chance, he will turn out to be a wonderful father. I never gave him that chance. That was my fault, and you are now paying for my mistake.

Bareeba and the doctors think that by sending you away, they are prolonging my life because I won't have to worry about making the many decisions that mothers continuously have to make like what you wear and how late you stay out—all those day-to-day things.

Tommy, I love being a part of those decisions. I *love* every minute of being your mother.

I agreed to send you to Jud this summer for two reasons: I wanted to make up for my past mistake while I still had time. But also, darling, I don't want you to see me getting weaker. I want you to remember me strong and young.

When you were three, Jud and I used to take you sailing in an old dinghy that he had fixed up with a mast. I would hold you, and you would tip your head back and laugh at the gulls and the sky, the sound of water rattling against the centerboard, the buoys and lobster pots. Holding you in my arms made me feel strong and secure, as if life had given me a second chance.

Tommy, I have my own reason for sending you away. I won't let you see me die.

I love you always and always,
Mom

CHAPTER
6

Several days passed. Jud moved the garbage pail into the shed. There were no more notes tacked to the door, but Clyde drove by in his jeep and said the dog was a menace to the peace of the neighborhood, and he for one wasn't going to stand for it.

"Like to see him try," growled Jud. "Most of the time he's too damn drunk to do anything but fall on his face."

Tommy didn't answer. She carried this last letter with her everywhere. All of a sudden, the dying had become very real. She felt as though her chest were being crushed slowly in a huge invisible vise.

Dozer snuffled his wet nose under her hand for a

pat. She stroked him and felt the tears building up behind her eyes. "I'm going up to my room," she said hurriedly and ran up the narrow stairs.

Jud followed slowly. Tommy could hear him clumping up the stairs, one heavy boot at a time. He knocked as he pushed open the door slowly. Tommy looked up from the bed where she had pushed her face into the pillow. "Jud, please don't send Dozer away. I can't bear it. I really can't. He's all I have from home that's alive!"

Jud sat down on the edge of the bed and rubbed his chin thoughtfully. "Tommy, I didn't say I was going to get rid of your dog. I know he's important to you. That's why I got him in the first place. I want you to be happy."

"How can I be happy?" shouted Tommy angrily. "Mommy's dying!"

"Yes. I know," said Jud in a low voice. "And I still . . . But look, I talked to Joe and sort of explained things. He said we could try Dozer at the yard. Just try him, mind you. If he bites one of the customers, then we'll have to figure something else out."

"You mean you're not going to send Dozer back to the kennel?" faltered Tommy.

" 'Course not." Jud shook his head. "Why would I do a thing like that? I can see how much that dog means to you."

"Jud?" Tommy asked slowly. "Could you teach me to sail?"

Dear Mom,

Dozer has become a "yard" dog. Every morning, he climbs into the jeep with me and Jud and drives to work. The only difference is he doesn't drink coffee out of marmalade jars.

Everyone pats him and gives him bits of their sandwiches. I'm afraid he's going to get quite fat at this rate.

He has his own schedule. Mornings, he's in the office with me. Lunch, he's outside going to all the men and begging for food. He doesn't bark or whine, he just stares and drools.

After lunch, he and Buddy lie side by side in the shade of some old scaffolding and nap. Jud bought Dozer a flea collar, just in case some of Buddy's fleas get the notion to migrate.

I love you, Mom. But I think you're wrong. This is the time when I want to be with you. Please change your mind and let me come home.

Love,
Tommy

P.S. I'm sorry my last letter sounded sad. I was upset about Dozer. But everything has worked out fine, and I promise not to write any more depressing letters. I want to make you happy.
P.P.S. Jud is teaching me how to sail!!!!!

"That's right, Tommy, easy does it."

Tommy squinted up at the sail, her fingers wrapped

tightly around the tiller. "It's all backward, Jud. When I pull the tiller this way, the boat turns the other way. Why can't it be like a car?"

"That's what your mother said when I first taught her. But she turned out to be quite a fine sailor— once she got the hang of it. Watch it now, you're starting to luff. See the sail shaking along the mast? Ease off a bit. That's right."

Tommy groaned. "There's so much to remember."

The water was a sparkling blue. A crisp breeze pushed against the sail, and the boat heeled slightly to one side. From the bow, Dozer turned and eyed them reproachfully.

Jud took the tiller, and Tommy leaned her head back and trailed her fingers in the icy water. The sky was so clean and clear it seemed to shimmer and glisten above her. She held up her hand and let the drops slide down her arm, leaving little slick paths of coldness on her skin. When she turned her head, she could see the shore; white granite boulders and gray rocks, a dark line of pine trees, or sometimes, where the shore was flatter, clumps of birches, their pale leaves twinkling like tiny stars in the distance. I wish I could feel this way always, thought Tommy.

The boat turned briskly, then slowed until it was almost standing still. The sails rattled and shook noisily. The boom banged back and forth. Waves angrily slapped against the bottom of the boat. Wind pummeled Tommy from all directions. "What's happening, Jud?" she asked in a frightened voice. Was the boat going to sink? Would she drown, floundering in the freezing Maine water?

"It's okay, Tommy," said Jud soothingly. "We just came about, that's all."

Then as the boat turned more, the wind kicked at the sail from the other side and the dinghy slid forward again.

"What do you mean?" persisted Tommy. The sail had filled, and her fear was receding. But still, what exactly had happened?

"We turned into the wind," answered Jud. "And when you do that, the wind comes right at you for a second. The sail luffs and the boom swings back and forth and the boat stops moving. Then you finish the turn, and the wind fills the sail from the other side. It's called tacking."

Tommy nodded. Sailing was fun, but there were a lot of new words to learn. They came about again, and this time it wasn't so scary. When the boat turned into the wind, she knew it was just part of changing directions.

She gave Dozer a shove. He had decided that the cooler was a good seat, and he was sprawled on top of it, panting and occasionally licking the salt off his paws.

"Hungry?" asked Jud.

Tommy nodded. "Yup."

"There's Counting Island right up ahead. Soon as we get close, we'll pull up the centerboard and land on the beach."

Tommy looked where he was pointing. A tiny island lay ahead—almost a doll's island. It had several small trees sprouting out of its center surrounded by low-growing bushes, a clearing, high granite boulders, and a small sandy beach. The whole island was certainly no larger than an acre.

The beach came rapidly closer. Jud let out the sail a bit. "Take the tiller, Tommy, and just keep us straight." He moved to the center of the boat and uncleated a line. He eyed the water and the shore. Then suddenly he yanked at the line.

Tommy heard a sliding sound as the centerboard lifted. Jud quickly cleated the line and scrambled back to take the tiller. He released the sail completely, but the momentum carried them forward until the sand rasped loudly against the underside of the boat.

Dozer was the first to disembark. He hung his head over the bow for a moment, before deciding that it was safe to leap out. Then giving himself a shake, he loped delightedly up and down the little beach. Soon he had found a piece of wood and was growling as he shook it back and forth in his teeth.

Tommy was next. The water was cold on her ankles, and the sand felt itchy under her toes. She walked gingerly up the shore to the high-tide line.

Jud carried the cooler. He didn't seem to mind the water sloshing over his work boots. He set the cooler down and gave a long, hard pull on the cleat that adorned the very tip of the bow. The dinghy heaved out of the water and rested on the beach—tipped to one side. "There. She won't drift away now. Tide's still coming in, but not for long."

After lunch, Tommy lay on her back with her arms stretched above her head. She closed her eyes and listened to a few tiny birds chirping in the shrubs and the waves lapping at the shore. A few feet away, Dozer was panting slowly in the heat of the afternoon. She sighed. "This is heaven," she murmured. She sat up and squinted at the water. "I'd much rather be here than in church."

"Church?" asked Jud. He put down his cigarette and eyed Tommy cautiously.

"Today *is* Sunday."

Jud frowned and looked at his cigarette. "Well, church is important, I guess."

"Do you ever go?" questioned Tommy.

"No," answered Jud truthfully. "But I kind of figure if God is everywhere, it doesn't really matter. I have informal chats with Him. I say, 'Should I do this?' and then another voice says 'Ayuh, Jud, that

seems like a good idea.' And then I figure it's the
right thing to do." He paused. "I like this island. I
think God likes it too, and I think He kind of smiles
whenever He remembers it."

Tommy tried to absorb this casual approach to
religion. How typical of Jud, she thought to herself, giving God a Maine accent. And yet she under-
stood what he was saying. That's the way Mom thinks
about God. Mom says it better though. She could
almost hear her mother's voice. "Look at the beauty
in each flower and each sunset—all the wonderful
things around you. That's what God is all about.
You can't see Him. But you can see the beauty. And
when I put my arms around you, and you feel all
safe and warm and loved, that's God too." Tommy
was seven then, and she still loved being hugged
and cuddled. No, not just when I was a child, she
reminded herself. Now! I want Mom to hug me *now*.
I wouldn't be embarrassed at all—ever again! She
blinked hard and pushed her hair behind her ears
with a single swipe. "Lida Barnaby says we should
go to church. More specifically, *I* should go to church
so that I can meet people my own age. Can you
believe that?" she questioned indignantly, her voice
brittle and tense.

Jud slowly twisted his cigarette into the sand and
then buried it with his forefinger. "Well, I been worried about that too," he said slowly. "I want you to
have friends."

Suddenly Tommy felt angry. "I don't need friends," she snapped. "I have enough to worry about without getting friends. Besides, I have plenty of friends back home. Plenty!"

Soon it was time to pack up the cooler and set sail back. Jud pushed the boat into the water and then clambered in, his boots dripping all over the floorboards.

"Are we going to . . . tack?" asked Tommy hesitantly.

Jud smiled a slow smile. "No. This is a run now for most of the way. The wind's behind us, and all we have to do is let the sail all the way out."

The water roared under the hull, but the boat was steady. "I think I like this better than tacking," said Tommy.

Jud laughed. "Well, most people would agree with you on that," he said.

My darling daughter,

I'm glad that Dozer is settling in. Be sure and find a local vet to keep up on his shots. It makes me happy to think of you learning to sail with Jud. It makes me remember so many things that I thought I had forgotten.

Soon after that first race, Jud began teaching me how to sail. We seemed to share so many things— we both loved to watch the gulls circling, and listen to the water slapping against the hull of the boat, and the feel of the cool wet breezes that pushed against the sails. It was our own world.

Jud was my only friend. Louisa had her own friends who she had "summered" with since she was two. Uncle George and Aunt Sissy were busy with their own friends—a hard-drinking older set, and that left me on my own.

Everyone liked Jud. He was tall, handsome, and he knew everything there was to know about boats. But he was a loner. The girls, even the summer girls, had crushes on him. He treated everyone with a cautious respect and a shy smile.

I set about learning everything I could about him. He was thirty-four years old, and if he had a girlfriend, no one at the Club knew about it. Finally, I asked him.

"No," he answered. "No girlfriend. I haven't found the right girl. And even if I have," he added in a low voice, "she's too young for me." Then he looked away. I couldn't help wondering if he meant me.

We went sailing together as often as he could get away from his duties. We still called it sailing lessons, but mostly we talked or watched the waves together. Sometimes our hands would rest on the tiller together—as if by chance, barely touching.

"You're spending a lot of time with Jud," said Louisa one day over breakfast.

"He's teaching me how to sail," I answered.

"Well, just remember, he's a local."

I nodded. I was beginning to understand the implication. Being a local meant the summer people could rave about how responsible he was and the summer girls could have secret crushes on him, but they would never dream of dating him.

The summer boys talked in furtive whispers about "local girls" they had kissed behind the clubhouse after closing time. Their conversation was filled with sordid exploits that made the summer girls listen eagerly, shivering discreetly with vicarious thrills.

But I wasn't part of the summer crowd. I felt uneasy when I was with Louisa's friends, as if I was playing a part. Somehow, it had been accepted as common knowledge that my father had retired from owning a steel mill. I did not deny this, and Louisa, if anything, promoted the charade. After all, she didn't want the houseguest of her parents to be the daughter of a plumber. There was talk of boarding school adventures. No, I decided to stay home, I explained, because my mother disapproved of girls being unchaperoned. It seemed that each time I spoke, another lie was dragged out of me.

Even with Jud, I was not completely honest. I shared a letter I had received from Pete. But I never spoke of my father or the tiny squalid house we lived in.

Still, Jud was my anchor. Whenever I couldn't stand Uncle George and Aunt Sissy's squabbling, I went sailing with Jud. And when I felt left out of Louisa's life, I searched for Jud. In fact, all I had to do was picture him in my mind, and I felt better.

To Jud, I was a summer girl—out of reach. Besides, he was seventeen years older than I.

Perhaps it was the age difference that made Uncle George and Aunt Sissy ignore the fact that we were spending so much time together. Their attitude was, How nice Jud is, trying to teach Elaine how to sail. Sometimes Uncle George would quiz me on the parts of boats. I would reply easily and quickly—because, actually, I *was* learning how to sail.

I was also falling in love.

                                                      Mom

By the end of July, the sun was so hot at lunch that every day, the men swam off the wharf to cool down. Tommy had tried this once, but the water was freezing, and the seaweed looked as if it would reach up and grab her. Besides, it made her hair all sticky and salty for the rest of the day. Jud didn't swim either. The two of them ate their lunch in silence flanked by Dozer and Buddy. Often Tommy brought a book and read while Jud just stared ahead as if not seeing the boat yard at all.

She had almost finished her yogurt when several drops of water landed on her legs. Tommy looked up impatiently. It was Chris. He was standing over her, his cutoff jeans sopping wet.

"Umm, Tommy? The T.Y.A.'s having a dance this Saturday night. I was wondering if you'd like to go?"

Chris shifted from foot to foot as he stood before Jud and Tommy.

Tommy put her yogurt down on her lap and then held the container lightly between her knees so the ever-attentive Dozer couldn't nudge it with his ever-wet nose. "I don't know. What's T. Y. A.?"

"Timberock Youth Association. Joe's going to be one of the chaperons," he said to Jud. "And there's going to be a live band for part of the time. It's from seven until nine-thirty."

Tommy frowned and dug her spoon into the blueberry preserves. She could feel her face turning bright red.

"Do you want to go?" persisted Chris. He had removed his large "boy" hands from his pockets and was hitting his fist against his palm nervously.

"I'll let you know tomorrow, okay?" she finally said.

Chris shrugged his shoulders. "Okay . . . I just thought you might like to do something . . . I mean go to a party. Well, see ya." Tommy glanced up and saw that Chris was blushing as he turned on his heel.

"Well?" said Jud. He had snapped out of his day-dream and was looking at her curiously.

Tommy drove her spoon angrily down to the bottom of the container. "I don't know. Okay? I mean I don't know anybody. I don't know what to wear. I don't even know how I'll get to this stupid party.

And besides, Chris is a jerk. If I walk in with him, people will think I'm a jerk too. That's all I need."

Jud fumbled in his pocket for a match. "Well, do you want to go?"

"I told you, I don't know," snapped Tommy.

Jud lit his cigarette thoughtfully. "Suppose I ask Lida Barnaby what these parties are all about—and what you're supposed to wear."

Tommy's eyes widened in horror. "Mrs. Barnaby?" she asked indignantly. "I would die of embarrassment. If you even mention this to Mrs. Barnaby, I swear I'll never speak to you again. And stop laughing at me!"

"I'm not laughing. I'm smoking," Jud replied seriously. But he turned away as he inhaled and coughed in a very untypical way. "All right, I won't ask Lida. But I will ask around. Don't worry. I won't mention your name. I'll act like *I'm* the one that wants to go. Okay?"

Jud was spared, however. When Tommy returned to the office, Joe Bartlett looked up from his ledger and grinned. "Coming to the dance, Tommy?" he asked. "Tell your dad it's nothing to worry about, me and my wife'll be there. I'm head of T.Y.A. The music is too damn loud for me, but the kids like it. And we have a live band coming. That's big for us. And everyone wears jeans. You could come like you are now and everyone would think you dressed special for the dance. What do you say?"

Tommy nervously shoved her hands into her pockets. "I don't know, maybe." She felt as if she was split in half. One half wanted to go to the dance and was already planning which jeans to wear and which shirt. Certainly *not* the jeans she was wearing at the moment. The other half wanted nothing to do with any of this.

Joe laughed. "I know that Chris asked you—which means that Jud drives you there. And you meet Chris on the steps. And then at nine-thirty sharp, Jud comes and gets you. T.Y.A. rule: A parent comes late and they have to be a chaperon next dance. I can't quite see Jud a chaperon, can you, Tommy?"

"I don't know," answered Tommy cautiously. After all Jud *was* her father. He *could* be a chaperon if he wanted to. Except it was horribly embarrassing to have your parents be chaperons at parties. Even back home, it just wasn't done.

Suddenly, she found herself wondering what Sheila was doing, and Peter Farber. Not one letter from either of them! Well, I'm not just going to stand around and wait, she thought angrily to herself.

Dear Mom,

No time to write. I'm going to a dance. It's given by T.Y.A., which is some kind of youth organization—kind of like what we have back home. Joe Bartlett says there will probably be some kids from the school I would be going to—if I stayed here through the winter. I told him no chance, I was going home in the fall.

Wish me luck. I'm a little scared. I wish you were here. I've never gone to a party without you telling me that I look nice. I'm wearing my black jeans.

Love,
Tommy

Tommy came down the stairs slowly. "Well, how do I look?" she asked Jud cautiously. She had tried to remember all of her mother's advice while getting ready. Easy on the mascara, no eyeliner, easy on the blush, and a conservative shade of lipstick—no fire-engine reds or browns. She had brushed her short blond hair behind her ear on one side so that her tiny diamond earrings could be seen. An oversized sweatshirt fell just below her hips.

Jud looked at her admiringly. "Terrific, Tommy. You look really great!" He stared closer. "Are you wearing makeup?"

Tommy scowled. "So?" She hoped he wouldn't be like Aunt Bareeba and call her a tart and make her wash it off.

"I've never seen you wearing makeup. You look good. It makes you look older, though. . . . Does your mother let you wear makeup?" Jud added slowly.

Tommy glared at him, anger surging up through her. How dare he question her right to wear makeup? How dare he even mention her mother?

But before she could think of a really cutting reply, she realized that he was just trying to be a parent and say the things that parents say. After all, he
didn't have a clue what kids were like. Her anger
dissolved just as quickly as it had appeared. "It's okay,
Jud," she said and grinned up at him. "I'm thirteen.
Mom lets me wear makeup so long as I don't overdo
it."

Jud sighed with relief. "Well, you look great."

All of a sudden, Tommy noticed that Jud was
looking pretty good himself. He must have gone
out to the barber while she was dressing and gotten
himself a shave and a haircut. He was wearing clean
pants, a comfortable-looking sweater with his collar
turned back over the top. He even had on shoes—
real shoes—*not* fish-smelling work boots. "You look
great too, Jud!"

A wave of misgiving washed over her. "You're not
going to be a chaperon, are you?" she asked suspi-
ciously.

Jud laughed. It was so strange to hear him laugh
that Tommy frowned in disbelief. It was such a
friendly, happy laugh. "Of course not!" he reassured
her. "I just didn't want you to be ashamed of me. So
I kind of spruced myself up. Hey, we'd better get
moving. That Chris fella will be wondering what
happened to you."

They didn't talk as they drove along. It was still
light, and the ten-mile trip seemed to take forever.

Tommy felt her heart begin to pound with appre-
hension as they approached the town . . . turned
down the street . . . saw the cars . . . and kids mill-
ing about in front of a large shingled building. . . .

"I just don't know anybody," she said in a low
voice.

"You'll do fine, Tommy. And that Chris is a nice
fella." Jud looked at his daughter, a worried expression in his eyes. "But if he gets fresh, you go find Joe
Bartlett. Maybe this dance wasn't such a good idea
after all."

They were at the steps. "I'll be fine," whispered
Tommy indignantly.

CHAPTER
7

Dear Mom,

I had a *great* time! Chris, he's the boy at the boat yard, looks a lot better when he's not covered in grease. He's a pretty good dancer too.

Joe Bartlett introduced me to a girl named Cathy who goes to the school that I would be going to—*if* I stayed here. She has red hair and freckles and is very nice. She said maybe we could go to the movies some time. She was impressed that Chris was my date. Apparently, a lot of girls really like Chris.

Chris is about my height. He's kind of cute. He's shier than Peter Farber, but that's good. Peter always tries to bully people into doing what he wants. There were only two slow dances. We sat out the first one. Chris said he was tired. But we danced the second one . . . . ! ! ! ! ! !

I wonder if I'm starting to like him? I wish you were here. You're always so good to talk to about these things.

Jud brought me in his truck. At first, I was kind of embarrassed because I was worried that everyone else would have cars, but there were just as many trucks. Joe Bartlett was on the steps saying hello to people, and Chris was talking with some friends.

We both got out of the truck. I was totally mortified, because most of the parents stayed in their cars. Chris saw us and came right over. He even shook Jud's hand. (I'm sure he's never done *that* at the yard) and then told me I was looking great.

Believe it or not, the dance was exactly like the dances we have at home! There were soda and pretzels at one side, a huge floor for dancing, and a number of adult chaperons. Most of them stood against the walls and looked uncomfortable.

Joe Bartlett, on the other hand, stuffed paper napkins in his ears and barreled about patting people on the back and joking. He looked like a huge rabbit with these white paper ears sticking straight out of his head. But the kids really like him. He kept introducing me to different people. I can't remember hardly any of their names, but everyone was really friendly.

It was almost like being back in Illinois.

Tommy rested her pen and let her mind relive the dance. . . . How afterward, she and Chris had walked slowly down the steps—their shoulders almost touching. The music had stopped, and Tommy could feel her ears ringing. "See you at work Monday," said Chris and grinned at her.

"I'm going to be pretty tired."

"Me too . . . Umm, Tommy, thanks for coming to the dance with me."

Tommy looked down at her sneakers. "Thanks for asking." Suddenly she glanced up and met his eyes. "I mean, really, thanks," she said sincerely. "I don't know anyone here, and if I *do* end up . . . living here . . . it's nice to have friends." She saw Jud's truck pull slowly up. "I'd better go. 'Bye," she added.

Jud leaned over and opened the door for her. "Well?" he asked anxiously.

"I had a terrific time!" she answered. She tipped back her head and pictured herself slow dancing with Chris. Then she wondered if Cathy was "best friend" material. There were so many things to think about!

As they entered the house, met by the ever-jubilant Dozer, she turned to Jud. "By the way, what did you do while I was at the dance?"

Jud looked down and drew a deep breath. "I circled."

"You what?"

"Well . . . I wasn't sure how things would go, and I wanted to be there in case . . . well, in case you needed me."

Tommy smiled. It was a little embarrassing to have

your father driving around and around the block for
two hours, but in some ways it was kind of nice.
"Thanks, Jud," was all she said.

My darling Tommy,

I'm so glad to know that you are settling in and
making new friends.

I didn't have any friends that first summer, except
for Jud. I didn't seem to need them. I had Jud.

July raced by and soon it was mid-August. Soon,
The Little Princess would sail back down the coast to
Maryland.

There was an end-of-the-racing-season dance at
the Yacht Club the night before we were scheduled
to leave. Even Jud was invited—as a guest! (Usually
he attended these functions as a hired bartender.)

We danced on the veranda that overlooked the
bay. The boats were twinkling with lights, the water
was black, and the sky was filled with millions of
stars.

Then we went for a midnight sail. Jud showed me
how the water sparkled with silver bits. Phospho-
rescence, he called it. I leaned back in the boat, trailed
my finger, and cut a tiny silver path in the cold still-
ness of the night bay.

"I leave tomorrow," I said quietly.

"I know." There was such pain in his voice.

I thought of returning home, to that awful room I
shared with Bareeba, to Poppa shouting at me, and

Momma just looking at me as if I had somehow betrayed her.

I thought of Jud, his kindness, the way he made me feel as if I was the most special person in the world, and I began to cry.

Jud put his arms around me. I clung to him, sobbing, and the boat rocked us both as gently as a cradle.

We eloped that night. A year later, you were born.

I'm a little tired now, Tommy. The doctor has started me on a new medication, which helps ease the pain, but it does make me sleepy. Some days are better than others. On the good days, I think that maybe I'm actually getting stronger!

Bareeba has been with me round-the-clock. We're closer now than we ever were when we were young. She is very patient with me.

I love you, darling, and think of you every day.

Mom xxxxooooo

Tommy threw down the letter angrily. How dare Aunt Bareeba "get close" to her mother now? I'm the one who should be there, she fumed. I'm the one who should be taking care of Mom round-the-clock.

"You all right, Tommy?" asked Jud anxiously.

"Fine, just fine," snapped Tommy. "And you know what? I hate Aunt Bareeba, and if I could find a way of killing her and not get sent to prison, believe me, I would!"

Jud nodded. "I know. She used to make me feel that way too. . . . Do you want to talk about it?" he added hesitantly.

"With you?" stormed Tommy. "Why? Where were you all those years when I needed a father? You never loved me. What did you ever do to Mom to make her leave you? She loved you so much!"

Jud rubbed his forehead with the back of his hand. "I don't know what to say, Tommy. I just don't know what to say."

"You never know what to say! You never say anything!"

"I don't mean to make you unhappy, Tommy." Jud's expression was anxious. "I know you bought a map from Henry Jallop. You're planning to run away, aren't you?"

"So now you're snooping in my drawers?" yelled Tommy.

"No, I didn't. Please, Tommy, Henry told me," pleaded Jud.

"Well, you're right. I think about running away. I think about running away all the time. I hate it here, and I hate you! What gives you the right to be my father after all this time? I don't blame Mom for leaving you!"

"You're right, Tommy. I . . ." Jud's voice was tired

and defeated. He fumbled in his pocket for his cigarettes and walked quietly out to the lawn.

"Typical!" stormed Tommy as she ran up the stairs to her room and slammed the door.

The next few days were workdays. Jud and Tommy did not really speak to each other except when absolutely necessary. A huge distance lay between them. Tommy felt a little guilty for screaming at Jud, when the person she was *really* angry with was Aunt Bareeba.

But Jud *was* in the wrong, she argued inside herself. He had never loved *her*. Fathers are supposed to "be there" for their children. She grew up with one faded photograph and a lot of stupid dreams.

My darling Tommy,

It is so hot here, you can hardly breathe. The lawn in front of our little house has turned yellow. Time seems to stand still.

There's something about August—it's always been a month of change for me. I married Jud in August. A week later, the news came that Pete had been killed. Four years passed, and I left Jud in August.

As Bareeba would say, "It's the heat that kills you, makes you crazy." Maybe she's right. Or maybe the heat brings thoughts and feelings you didn't know you had boiling up to the surface until it spills over

the edge—like a pot of vegetable soup when the flame
is up too high.

At first we were so happy. I moved in with Jud in
his rented room above the general store in Surry.
The season was almost over, so it didn't matter that
Jud was asked to resign his position at the Yacht Club.

Uncle George and Aunt Sissy were furious. They
never came back to Wink's Cove. The shame was
unendurable. Their houseguest, a relation (although
distant), had eloped with a local! The gossip! The
humiliation! Aunt Sissy almost suffered another of
her famous nervous breakdowns. From then on, in
deep disgrace, they summered in Castine.

Momma and Poppa disowned me. Bareeba flew up
to Maine and tried to convince me to annul the marriage. She flew back to Green River, violently angry
that she had failed.

Jud had no family to either support or condemn
the marriage. His mother had died when he was
young, and his father had died the year before.

We didn't need friends or family that first winter.
We had each other. We sailed in Jud's dinghy until
the November snows began to fall. Then we took
long walks on empty winding roads. My whole world
consisted of Jud.

Then came the summer. I was pregnant. Jud was
working two jobs—as a carpenter in a boat yard at
night, and as a cashier in an all-night supermarket in
Ellsworth.

At the beginning of August, he surprised me with

a little house on the shore. He had gone terribly in debt to buy it, but he said nothing was too good for his "summer girl." "Summer girl," that was what he called me.

You were born August 30th. Another August change.

The summer people left. That winter was hard. I had a baby to care for. Jud worked overtime whenever he got the chance. It was very lonely. I began to try and make friends. But the local people thought of me as "summer." They were courteous, they smiled at me, but they were always distant.

The following summer, I tried to reestablish the tentative friendships that I had begun when I was visiting the Crandalls. But the summer people considered me a "local." They too were courteous, at least to my face, but I was never included in their activities.

All the while, the money problems were escalating. The mortgage on the house, taxes, fuel bills. I was desperately lonely for friends. "Each other" was no longer enough. Jud was overworked. I was depressed. Soon it seemed that the only thing we shared in common was you.

You were such a pretty baby. Jud used to take you with him whenever he could. He was so proud of you. Everyone loved you, summer people and locals alike. Everyone wanted to hold you and tickle you and make you laugh. Even the summer people would give you lovely presents. And the crabbiest old lob-

sterman would suddenly dive into his pocket and bring
out a beautiful carved wooden bird or whistle for
you to play with.

But while you made friends wherever you went, I
couldn't live *through* you. I needed my own life.

Jud was away so much, and when he was home,
all we talked about was you. That little house on the
shore became a prison. I was only twenty-one—the
year when most people are beginning their adult life,
and already I felt as if my life was over.

You were three that last summer. I took a house-
keeping job for Allen Kingston. The Kingstons had
always summered in Blue Hill. They had a beautiful
house on the shore, with acres and acres of woods,
velvet green lawns, and gardens of flowers surround-
ing the house. Mr. and Mrs. Kingston were traveling in Europe.

Their only son, twenty-four-year-old Allen, was
staying in the house—on strict orders not to get into
trouble. Then the family housekeeper broke her leg.
Allen advertised in the local paper. I applied for the
job. Allen hired me on the spot and said I could
bring you with me to work.

The pay was generous. It seemed to be the solu-
tion to our problems, the answer to our prayers. Jud
even took me out to dinner to celebrate. And afterward, that evening, we were closer than we had been
for months.

At first, everything went well. While I scrubbed
and polished, you played in the garden. You had

struck up a friendship with the ancient gardener, and the two of you became inseparable. His name was Bert. You called him "Uncle Birdie."

Allen Kingston rarely left the house. He mostly lounged by the pool and read. He said I could take you swimming after work whenever I liked. The pool was heated, and it seemed to be the perfect opportunity to teach you how to swim. Jud was already taking you sailing with him whenever he got the chance.

As the summer progressed, Allen and I became friends. It was wonderful to *have* a friend. My salary helped pay the bills. Jud became more relaxed at home, more like the Jud I had fallen in love with. Everything was perfect. Then August came.

It seems so long ago. Please write and tell me more about the dance and this boy, Chris. I want to picture you happy, with friends.

I love you with all my heart,
Mom

Tommy stayed home from work. Her throat was sore, her head ached, and she could tell from the tingly feeling in her arms and stomach that she had a fever. Jud was reluctant to leave her alone and, in fact, only agreed to do so if Lida Barnaby checked up on her.

"Ayuh, you have a fever all right," said Mrs. Barnaby as she put her large squashy hand over

Tommy's forehead. "You should take Tylenol for it. I prefer aspirin myself, but they say Tylenol is safer on the stomach. Are you whoopsing, dear?"

"No, I just have a sore throat," replied Tommy with as much dignity as possible. "And I already took some Excedrin."

"I brought you some Jell-O. My boys always liked Jell-O when they were feeling poorly, but it had to be the red kind. Jell-O isn't Jell-O unless it's red. That's what they used to tell me. Now what's wrong with your father? I haven't seen him look so glum in years. Of course, he always looks a little glum since your mother left," she added thoughtfully.

"I guess he doesn't like being a father," snapped Tommy. "Just because my mother left him, he could have written me or tried to see me. Do you know how hard it is to come and visit—maybe even *live* with a man you don't know, who obviously doesn't love you a bit?"

Mrs. Barnaby put both her hands on the table and looked hard at Tommy. "Now you wait a minute, young lady. Your father loves you very much. He always has."

Tommy winced as she swallowed. It felt like there were knives in her throat. "Mrs. Barnaby, I'm not a child. Fathers who care see their children or write to them. It's as if I didn't exist for the last ten years."

"Have you ever set foot in your father's room?"

"Of course not," snapped Tommy. Her head was *really* aching now.

"Well, I suggest you do so," said Mrs. Barnaby. "You're not giving poor Jud the chance he deserves. And he doesn't need to have his heart broken a second time either. . . . The water's on for some tea. I promised him I'd look out for you." With that, Lida Barnaby swept out of the room. The front door banged shut behind her.

I hate nosy, interfering busybodies, thought Tommy when the house was still again. She poured herself a cup of boiling water and impatiently bounced the tea bag up and down. Well, why not? I'll look in his room. There's no reason why I shouldn't. He never told me not to. "What do you say, Dozer?" From under the kitchen table, Dozer thumped his tail.

Tommy took a quick sip of her tea, which burned her mouth, and set the cup on the kitchen table. She approached the door to Jud's room slowly. She could feel the blood rushing into her cheeks, her heart pounding, and a sick prickly feeling in her stomach. "I'm not doing anything wrong," she told herself. She glanced quickly at the door as if she expected Jud to come driving back from work, or Lida Barnaby to pull into the weedy driveway.

She turned the knob and gave the door a push.

She was almost disappointed when it swung open. She had thought it might be locked.

The room was dark, too dark to see anything at first. A pine tree grew outside the window, so close to the house that its dark branches bristled against the windowpanes, blocking out all light. The room was small, dark, and gloomy. The single bed was unmade, its sheets and blankets in a tangle. Yesterday's work pants hung over a chair; the shirt had fallen in a crumpled heap to the floor.

Slowly, Tommy's hand found the light switch. As she flicked it on, light shot out of the overhead fixture and filled the room with a bright electric glare. Then she gasped in surprise.

Everywhere she looked there were pictures and mementos of . . . herself. But they were not just baby pictures. There were pictures of her fifth birthday party. She recognized the swing set decorated with a huge pink ribbon. In another, she was dressed as a pilgrim for the fourth-grade Thanksgiving play. Several neatly framed paintings, representing early and recent artwork, were spaced about. "I don't understand," she whispered.

She backed slowly out of the room, leaving the door open. She sipped the tea, now cold, and curled her feet up in an old armchair in the living room.

When she next became aware of her surroundings, hours had passed. She ate some Jell-O. The door to Jud's room was as she had left it, open. She gave the area a wide berth as she walked to the kitchen. Her head and throat ached horribly now. Her Excedrin and throat lozenges were upstairs. It seemed like too much effort to get them, even though she knew they would make her feel better. She crept back into the armchair and pulled her robe around her.

She opened her eyes as she felt arms lift her. "Tommy, you're burning up!" There was concern in Jud's voice.

"My throat is sore," she whispered and leaned her head against Jud's chest, feeling safe and comfortable. She focused on the heavy clumping of his work boots as he carried her up the stairs. Gently, he tucked her into bed.

Tommy struggled to sit up. "Jud," she whispered, "I don't understand. Why do you have all those pictures of me in your room?"

"You're my daughter," answered Jud, as if that explained everything.

The next day, Jud stayed home from work. He made Tommy stay in bed and brought her ginger ale and soup on a tray. Dozer felt left out unless he was allowed to sprawl on the foot of Tommy's bed. Occasionally, Tommy slipped him one of her saltines, which he snapped up with gusto.

By afternoon, her fever had started to come down.

"It's just the flu," she explained to Jud. "I'm going to be perfectly fine."

Jud shook his head. "You sure had me worried, Tommy."

Tommy rearranged her pillows. "Jud, I have to ask you something."

Jud looked warily at her. "What?"

"I don't understand why you have all those pictures of me."

Jud sighed and looked away. "Well," he answered slowly, "for a long time, they were all I did have."

"But you never wrote me or let *me* know that you . . . cared about me."

Jud rubbed his chin. "Well, I know. See, when your mother ran off with that Kingston fella, I was pretty hurt. I didn't know what to do. The divorce papers said I was cruel to your mom. 'Mental cruelty.' That's what the papers said. I never meant to be cruel in any way. I would never hurt your mom. She was my life. You and her were the only things that mattered to me. Then she took you away. That Kingston fella had his lawyer send me something that said I was to stay away from you because I was an unfit father. I guess I kind of went crazy. I couldn't work, I couldn't sleep. Lida Barnaby took care of me—sort of like a big sister she was. And then before I knew it about three years had passed. I felt ashamed of the way I had turned out. Your mom kept sending me these pictures of you, and you looked so happy. I just felt you'd be better off without me in your life."

Tommy felt the tears slipping down her face. "Jud, do you know how many times I really *needed* a father?"

Jud ran his fingers through his white hair. His voice was slow. "I took real good care of all the things your mom sent me. I was proud to think of you growing up so pretty and smart. I'd try and picture you at school and with your friends."

"Why didn't you write or call?" persisted Tommy.

Jud shrugged his shoulders. "Well, I ain't much to look at, am I? Ellen at Dunkin' Donuts hit the nail on the head; I look more like your grandfather. I just didn't want you to be ashamed of me. I knew the other fathers would be young and making lots of money working in banks and offices. . . . I never deserved someone as good as your mom. She was way out of my reach, a summer girl. I don't blame her for leaving me. . . . I know that you'll leave me soon too. I knew that when I saw you get off the plane that first day—looking so pretty and so much like your mother. I won't stop you or get in your way. I promise."

"Oh, Jud." Tommy shook her head in exasperation. "I'm not going to run away. I don't have enough money anyway. It just made me feel better to pretend that I could."

Jud frowned. "I can't expect you to accept me as

a father now," he said. "You were right about that when you got mad the other day. I let you down as a father. But I'll stand by you like a friend, and I won't ask for more."

"I wasn't so much mad at you, as mad at Mom for being sick, and Aunt Bareeba for taking care of her," explained Tommy apologetically.

Jud patted her shoulder clumsily. "Well, that's okay. Let's start all over again."

Tommy nodded and grinned as Dozer lumbered up from the bottom of the bed to receive his pat also.

CHAPTER
8

Darling Tommy,

I married Allen at the end of August.

As I write these letters, I wonder how much should I share with you about my life? As I write, I remember things that I thought I had forgotten, and sometimes I find myself confessing things that I thought I had hidden forever.

Are these letters really for you? Or are they for me? Or both of us. I thought at first that my purpose was to give you a better understanding of Jud, but I'm the one who has gained understanding.

The time is short now, Tommy. I can see it in Bareeba's face and in the way the doctors touch me.

I can feel it in my body. Yet when I write to you, I live again. I walk and breathe and touch and feel all the things I ever cared about, and then time stretches out forever.

Please see me as a person as well as your mother, and please forgive me.

It was August. The sky was unbearably blue, and the ground screamed for rain. Great cracks opened up in the fields. The roads were dry and dusty. While you followed after Uncle Birdie in the back gardens, I swam in the pool with Allen. We played and splashed like children, and afterward in the cool shade of the pool house, I welcomed him.

Every day it was the same. I still loved Jud, but it was almost as if I had become two people: Allen's mistress, and Jud's wife.

Perhaps if Uncle Birdie and you had not seen us, it might have ended when Allen returned to Chicago. The summer was almost over. But one day, as Allen and I lay by the pool, I looked up, and there, over the hedge, was your innocent face staring at me. Uncle Birdie's face was ashen. He was trying to turn you away. But you held out your hands and said "Mommy?" in your questioning voice.

I knew then that I had to make a choice. Allen said I should leave with him immediately and become Mrs. Allen Kingston. He promised that you should go to the finest schools and wear the finest clothes.

"What about Jud?" I wept.

"Divorce him." Allen's answer was clear and quick. "He'll never forgive you. And it's bound to get back to him through Bert. The locals always gossip. Then he'll be the one doing the divorcing, and he'll take Tommy away from you. You'll never see her again. But it's your choice, Elaine."

"Divorce?" I asked, numb at the thought of losing you.

"My lawyers will handle it," he snapped. "Now I'll drive you back to your house so you can get your things, and we'll be on the plane before Jud returns. It's the only way. Sometimes it's kindest to be cruel."

I packed our things and left a note for Jud saying that I was marrying Allen and could not face his anger. I assured him that I had loved him when I married him, but that things had changed between us. I never saw him again.

The divorce went through quickly. I signed the papers that Allen gave me without reading them. We married immediately and presented his parents with the news when they returned from Europe.

Why did Allen marry me? It wasn't for love. Nor did I love him. I realize now that for him, it was the thrill of doing something that his parents would really disapprove of. After all, I was the housekeeper. I was married to someone else. Furthermore, he had the challenge of stealing me away from Jud, whom he had known since he was a child and had been jealous of.

I learned later that my leaving destroyed Jud. For months he raged. It was as if he lost his mind. His hair turned white. His clothes became tattered. He began sleeping on the shore. Finally Lida Barnaby took him in and cared for him. I sent her money to help with the medical bills. He was suffering from a physical collapse as well as a mental one. I should have come home then, but I didn't.

The marriage to Allen was not happy. I soon discovered that he drank heavily. He quickly lost interest in me and traveled often on "business trips."

Mr. and Mrs. Kingston tried their best to accept me and gave you lovely presents. They were kind people, and I hated myself for being the cause of their disappointment.

Technically, the marriage lasted three years. Actually, it was over as soon as it began. When Allen asked for a divorce, I freely gave it to him and asked for nothing in return. Bareeba was furious. She felt I was entitled to a large alimony for all my suffering. But I had not suffered, not really, because I had never loved Allen. I was drawn to him, yes. He was young, and rich, and represented all the things I thought I could never have. But I never loved him.

His parents gave me the little house we live in now. It's far from Chicago and Allen, and it's even farther from Maine. They were kind and supportive during the divorce proceedings. They still are. Each Christmas a lovely present arrives for you from Grandma and Grandpa Kingston.

Yesterday, Mrs. Kingston came and sat by my bed. I have not seen her in several years. She seemed older and quite frail. She held my hand and told me how sorry she was that her son had ruined my life. She said that she always considered you to be her first grandchild and that they kept a picture of you on their dresser. I told her how much her kindness had meant to me through the years. I told her not to feel badly about Allen. My life was my own, and the mistakes that I had made were my responsibility.

We've always had such fun in our little house. When I can't sleep, I look out the window and watch the leaves making patterns. Remember? You used to say that the tree was full of happy faces looking in at the window. I never knew what you meant. I can see them now.

> I love you so much.
> Mom

Jud looked at Tommy over his Dundee marmalade jar full of coffee. "You've got a birthday coming up next week."

"How'd you know?" asked Tommy.

"Last week in August. How could I forget? And this time I'm going to do it right. What do you want? Lida Barnaby says I can't go wrong with clothes, but I think if I was to pick them, I would. A new TV or a record player or something?"

Tommy looked away. "Jud," she answered slowly in a low voice. "There is something I want more than anything in the world. I want to see Mom."

Dear Mom,

By the time you get this letter, I will be home. Jud says better not warn Bareeba or we'll find the National Guard outside our house. I think he's right.

So tomorrow, I'll be with you again. I'm so happy I could burst.

I love you. xxxxooooo
Tommy

"No, you can't come in!" screeched Bareeba. "I'm in charge here, Tamara, and your mother is resting."

"She's *my* mother," snapped Tommy.

"Well, I'm not letting you in. It's against your mother's wishes. And you, Jud Foster, what are you doing here? Elaine never wants to see you again. You ruined her life . . . you . . . you. . . ." gasped Bareeba as she tried to think of a really dreadful name to call Jud.

"Get out of the way, Barbara," said Jud firmly, and he took Bareeba by the shoulders and practically lifted her up before dumping her in a chair. Tommy glanced at him in admiration. It took a strong man to move Aunt Bareeba.

"I'm calling the police! This will kill your mother, Tamara! Her death will be on your head."

"You interfere with my daughter and you can worry about your own death," growled Jud.

But Tommy had already run past her aunt and her father and up the stairs to her mother's bedroom.

"Tommy!" Elaine reached out her hands. She was very thin now, and her skin had a yellowish tint to it. Her voice was soft and weak.

Tommy ran and wrapped her arms around her. She rested her head against her mother's chest for a moment without saying anything. She felt her mother stroke her hair the way she always did when Tommy was a child. "Oh, Mommy, I've missed you so much. Is it okay that I came?" She lifted her head and stared into her mother's face.

"More than okay, darling. You've made this the happiest day of my life."

Tommy heard someone enter the room. She braced herself for Bareeba and did not turn her head.

"Hello, Elaine."

Tommy saw a warm, gentle expression come into her mother's face. It seemed that her cheeks even flushed a little.

"Jud. You haven't changed a bit," she said softly.

As Tommy watched her mother gaze wonder-ingly at Jud, she realized with amazement that her mother was seeing the Jud from the letters—the tall, handsome man with whom she had fallen in love. And Jud was looking back at her in adoration. "Neither have you, Elaine. Neither have you."

For a while they just stared at each other. To Tommy, it was as if ten years had vanished and they were a family again. She found herself smiling and wanting to cry all at the same time.

"Now, Tommy," Elaine said, with a trace of fun in her voice, "I want to hear all about this Chris, and your new job at the boat yard, and the dance. It sounds like so much fun. I don't want to miss a single detail!" Her fingers closed around Tommy's hand, while her other hand reached out to take Jud's.

So, as the hot August sun beat down on the house, the three of them spent the afternoon laughing, planning the future, and . . . remembering.

◆

The funeral service was small. Jud and Tommy sat in the front pew, aware of the minister's voice but not really listening to the words.

Afterward, as they walked from the cemetery, Tommy found her thoughts slipping back to her mother's letters—the sun on the water, the sea gulls, the craggy granite shore. There was work at the boat yard, Dozer was lonely, her new friend Cathy had asked her to go shopping at the mall, and of course there was Chris . . . .

She touched Jud's hand. "Come on, Dad. It's time to go home."

DEBORAH MOULTON

has written two highly praised books of fantasy for young adult readers, *The First Battle of Morn* and *Children of Time*, both published by Dial.

Ms. Moulton has spent many summers in Maine where, like Tommy and her parents in *Summer Girl*, she learned to love sailing. Ms. Moulton now lives with her husband and two children in Southampton, New York.

25 - 3/01
07/02 - ✓